The Legend of Thunderfoot

The Legend of Thunderfoot

BILL WALLACE

ALADDIN PAPERBACKS
New York · London · Toronto · Sydney

❧ ALADDIN PAPERBACKS

An imprint of Simon & Schuster Children's Publishing Division

1230 Avenue of the Americas, New York, NY 10020

Copyright © 2006 by Bill Wallace

All rights reserved, including the right of reproduction

in whole or in part in any form.

ALADDIN PAPERBACKS and related logo are registered trademarks of Simon & Schuster, Inc.

Also available in a Simon & Schuster Books for Young Readers hardcover edition.

Designed by Jessica Sonkin

The text of this book was set in Lomba.

Manufactured in the United States of America

This edition specifically printed for school book fairs by Simon & Schuster.

10 9 8 7 6 5 4 3 2 1

CIP data for this book is available from the Library of Congress.

ISBN-13: 978-1-4169-5390-6

ISBN-10: 1-4169-5390-6

*To Kaden Keith and Jordan Paige Wallace
and William James Moore*

Old Friends

It was a slow process. For each step he took, his friend took ten. It seemed as if they'd been walking all night, but at his age there was no longer the need to get anywhere in a hurry.

"How much farther?" he asked.

"We're almost there."

"That's what you said the last time."

"If you don't like my answer—quit asking."

"It's dark. Roadrunners aren't supposed to be out walking around in the dark. We're supposed to be hiding or sitting in a tree."

"Stop griping. The moon's almost full. You can see just fine. Besides, when have you ever done *anything* a roadrunner's *supposed* to do?"

At the top of a short hill, the tortoise stopped. There were two mesquite trees, one with a wide trunk, the other with a fallen limb.

"This is it," he whispered. "We can hear from behind this one, and they won't see us."

"Why wouldn't you just tell me? Why did we have to come clear over here and . . ."

The tortoise shushed him. "You have to hear this for yourself. I've lost track of the times I've heard it. With each telling, the story gets bigger and more outlandish. This was the first opportunity I was close enough to find you and get you back in time. If I had tried to tell you, you wouldn't have believed me."

"When have I ever doubted you?"

The tortoise's neck arched so he could look back over his shell. His expression was enough to hush the roadrunner. Side by side, they stood behind the wide trunk of the mesquite. "Here come the young roadrunners," the tortoise whispered. "Set your tail feathers down and hush."

A tiny orange sliver peeked above the mountains in the east. Mother roadrunner at his side, the father hopped onto a tall rock and looked down at his three children.

"Today is the time of The Naming! When the bottom of the sun touches the mountains, I will tell you the legend," the father announced to the children who

stood in front of him. "After you have heard the legend, you will go—one at a time—to find food. Your mother and I will watch. We will see your speed, agility, cunning, alertness, and determination. When you return here, your name will be given, and you will begin a life of your own."

"That's not the way it works," the old roadrunner whispered, peeking around the trunk of the tree. "When the bottom of the sun touches the mountains, *that* is the time of The Naming. They're doing it all wrong. There's no legend."

The old tortoise glanced up at him. "There is now, at least outside your precious Paradise Valley. That's what I wanted you to hear. Hush."

They waited. Watched the sun as it slowly inched its way toward the sky. The instant the bottom of the sun rested on the mountain peaks, the father spoke.

"The story I tell is more than a story. It is legend! It was passed to me from my father. You will pass it to your children, from now until the end of time. It is the legend of the greatest roadrunner who ever lived. Great not only because of his great size, but great because of his great deeds.

"The great one was born fully grown. His parents did not fledge him. He fledged himself on the very day he hatched. He hunted by high sun—so hungry and so good at finding food he brought dragonflies, tarantulas, even rabbits back to his family.

"By the time he was three sunrises, he was as big as his mother and father put together. His wings were so powerful he could fly high in the sky. He could soar as the eagle. He had legs so strong he could chase down a coyote.

"Predators feared him. They even feared the place where he and his mate lived. We call it Paradise Valley. The coyotes and bobcats call it the Valley of Doom. Whenever predators venture there, mystic stones fall from the clear blue sky. They crash so close that it strikes terror in the predators' hearts. Sometimes rocks strike them. Only the foolish or the nonbelievers dare to go there. But if they do and the mystic stones do not drive them away, the great one and his mate will.

"Two coyotes ventured into his valley. He ran them down. He struck them with his huge feet, driving their heads into the sand. His claws were so strong he once picked up a bobcat, flew her into the sky, and dropped her. She fell from such a height she was buried in the sand—never to be seen again.

"No roadrunner has ever been hit by one of these mystical stones. No roadrunner has ever been harmed in this place called Paradise Valley. For roadrunners, there is no danger there. The food is plentiful.

"In Paradise Valley the great one grew and grew. His huge, sharp claws became strong as steel. Each time they strike the ground, sparks fly. We call this lightning. *The sound of his huge feet pounding the desert floor is so loud it rumbles through the canyons and shakes the very earth itself. We call this* thunder."

The old roadrunner blinked, shook his head, and looked down at the tortoise beside him. "Are you listening to this? Can you believe what that father is telling his kids? They're talking about *me*, aren't they?"

The old tortoise glanced up. His friend's eyes were so wide they looked as if they might pop clear out of his head.

"Yes. I always thought you were the stuff of legend, kid. Guess I was right."

"But this is ridiculous. I was just like any other roadrunner. And nobody ever got hit with a rock . . . and—"

"How about the bobcat?" the tortoise interrupted.

"Tess?"

"Yeah," the tortoise said with a nod. "What about her?"

"She was the most bullheaded cat I ever saw. Took us three seasons before she caught on that she wasn't wanted. Besides I didn't drop that rock. That was my wife. And it was an accident. Her aim has improved a lot since then, and . . ." He stopped a moment and sighed. "And as far as my feet . . . well . . . that didn't happen until . . . well, it was the day before The Naming. It was all because of that dumb old grasshopper. Remember?"

Chapter 1

The young bird had never been so excited. Never so nervous.

Tomorrow was The Naming.

The day his parents would give him his name. The Naming was the time all roadrunners left the safety of their parents' nests and struck out on their own. The time they no longer had to depend on anyone for food or protection. The time they would explore their range, meet other roadrunners, and establish their own territory. The time they would prove their courage, alertness, and skill as hunters—not just to themselves, but to the whole world. It was a proud time. A time he had longed for.

He felt right happy with himself. This finding food stuff was getting easier every day. Standing perfectly still, he listened, watching with sharp eyes from beneath the shade of a creosote bush.

Let's see, he thought. *Five grasshoppers, a lizard, two scorpions, and one skink tail. Well,* he thought with a shrug, *I should have had the whole skink. Daddy told me to grab them by the neck or back. If you grab them by the tail, it breaks off. The skink gets away, and you're left with nothing but a beakful of tail.*

But if Daddy had told him the truth, skinks' tails would grow back after a few months. *Next time I'll remember and get the whole thing.*

He fluffed his feathers, continued to watch and listen. A movement on the far side of some rocks caught his attention. There was a stand of weeds and short prairie grass. He could see just the very tops of the taller weeds and a saltbush above the rock. He froze. Completely motionless, he didn't even breathe.

A grasshopper.

Another leaped from the grass onto a broad leaf. Then another crawled up a wide stalk.

He flipped his long tail feathers. *A few grasshoppers ought to just about fill me up. Then I can go home and tell Mama, Daddy, and my sister how much I caught to eat. Maybe tomorrow, they will give me a strong name. A fast name, fitting a roadrunner.*

Maybe Speedy. Maybe Muscles or Dash or . . .

He felt a tingling when the feathers of his head crest sprang up. *Hunter! Yeah, Hunter would be a great name. Hunter. The world's greatest hunter.*

He started to make his sprint toward the grasshopper supper, then suddenly, remembering, he froze.

Roadrunners had rules. Like "always look before you leap!" Since the first day he'd left the nest on his wobbly legs, that's what Mama and Daddy told him and his sister. "Always look before you leap."

Make sure there are no coyotes, bobcats, or rattlesnakes around. If you look over an area before you go there, it's hard for a predator to sneak up on you. Of course, there *was* a second rule for roadrunners. "If a bobcat or coyote does sneak up on you, forget the rules! RUN!"

Flying was hard. It was much easier to walk. And running was . . . well . . . for a roadrunner, why walk if you can run? But "always look before you leap" was a little tough for him to remember. Sometimes when he was hungry, or when he was thinking about how to impress his mom and dad so he would get a good name, he forgot.

Quiet and easy, he put his foot back on the ground. His eyes stood out on each side of his head, so he could look not only in front of him, but to the sides and behind. He watched for the slightest movement.

Coyotes were usually easy to spot. They moved, trotting along or walking to search for mice, mesquite seeds, or cactus pods. Bobcats were sneaky. They usually lay in wait behind a rock or beneath a bush. But even at that, if he took the time to look, he would notice their whiskers twitching or the breeze ruffling their fur.

Once he was sure the area was clear, he darted from the shade of the creosote bush into the open. About halfway to the weeds where the grasshoppers were, he froze again.

A movement to the side caught his sharp eye. There was a white thing. The skull of a cow, parched by years in the bright sun and polished smooth by the desert wind and sand. The movement came from inside. There was straw there. A mother mouse scampered around, frantically sniffing and searching.

"My children!" she squeaked. "Where are my children?"

Another movement. A young mouse scampered from the pile of rocks near the grasshoppers. Running in a zigzag, he scurried across the sand

and into the cow skull. "A snake, Mama. He bit Wiggles and Squeakie. We ran for the rocks, like you told us to do. But they fell down and couldn't get up. The snake ate them."

"Where are Snout and Bouncy?" The mother poked her head out the nose hole of the skull and looked about.

"We're here." Two more mice darted from the rocks and into the skull. A grasshopper fluttered from a prickly pear to the stalk of an Apache plume, just behind them. For a second, the road-runner thought about the mice. They were tasty and filling, but he had his mouth set for a nice, juicy grasshopper.

Without another thought of the poor mice, he ran, crouching low so the rocks would shield his approach. Once there, he straightened. The fattest grasshopper chewed on a saltbush leaf beneath a clump of the large papery-looking seed wings.

In the blink of an eye, he sprang to the top of the rock. The grasshopper jumped, but it was too slow. The roadrunner grabbed it before it even cleared the leaf. Holding it in his beak for a second, he waited until the thing spit that nasty, foul-smelling tobacco juice, then crunched and swallowed it down.

A second grasshopper jumped from another branch and spread its wings to fly. It took the roadrunner two steps and a quick leap to catch it—in midair.

Now, where's that third one?

The last grasshopper sat at the top of a long, slender blade of buffalo grass. But just as the roadrunner darted toward it, the thing jumped. He slid to a stop in the loose sand, leaned sharply to the right, and charged after the grasshopper again. The thing landed on a baby barrel cactus. Just as he lunged to snap it up, it flew off to the left.

He turned and chased after it once more. After about five tries, he was getting just a bit ticked. "Some roadrunner you are," he muttered to himself. "Can't even catch a grasshopper. Guess the name Hunter is out. I can't believe this stupid bug's given me the slip. It's always just one step—or jump—ahead of me."

He made another stab at the grasshopper. Missed again. Buzzing its wings, the bug flew about six feet and disappeared behind a round rock.

Without giving the grasshopper a chance to rest or bend those knobby knees so it could spring again, he darted across the open ground, leaped clear over the rock, and landed on the other side.

There was no buzz. There was no rattle. Just a thump. A sudden pressure, as if a heavy twig had sprung back and hit the top of his toes.

Mama and Daddy had told him that rattlesnakes always rattle before they strike. Guess Mama and Daddy never landed on one.

Then the pain hit.

Chapter 2

His first thought was to run. He'd landed right on top of the baby rattler, and the smartest thing to do would be escape before it bit him again. Trouble was, the pain in his toes made him mad.

He jumped to the side. Only then did he hear the buzzing rattle. It was a faint sound. The young snake had only one little nub at the tip of its tail instead of a full set of rattles. Still the tail quivered fast as the desert wind in a sandstorm. The snake began to coil.

He and his sister had watched Mama catch a snake before. First she used her wings, one at a time, to distract the thing. When it struck at the moving wing, she dodged and grabbed it by the tail. Then she flung it through the air—over and over against the rocks—until it stopped moving.

"We roadrunners are the only birds who are quick enough and brave enough to eat rattlesnakes. Even so, wait until you are fully grown," she'd warned them. "And never bite off more than you can chew."

When they'd asked her what "never bite off more than you can chew" meant, Mama explained that if they tried to catch a snake that was too big or too strong, it would bite them. "If a rattlesnake bites you, you're a goner."

"Even a baby rattlesnake?" he'd asked.

"The poison from the babies is just as dangerous as the grown-up snake's. Be quick! Don't ever let one bite you!"

He was *not* fully grown. He didn't even have his name yet. But he had already been bitten. Besides that, he was really mad. So before the thing could coil, he grabbed its tail with the tip of his long, sharp beak and yanked!

The jerk was so hard and quick the rattler popped up as straight as a yucca leaf. When the roadrunner let go, it flew through the air. There was a sudden *thud* when it slammed against the round rock. Stunned, it lay perfectly still, but for only an instant. Then its head rose from the ground, mean and angry looking. Quickly its body began to coil. It hadn't even twisted into the second loop before he grabbed the tail again and yanked.

This time the snake spun through the air and landed on a small branch of the Apache plume. The little limb bowed low beneath its weight. Then when the branch could go no farther, it sprang back. The rattler flew high into the air. Straight and stiff, it spun about three times, then landed in the sand so hard that the dust flew.

"I may be a goner," the roadrunner clattered. "But so are you. In fact, I think I'll eat you for supper. My last meal."

The snake had barely raised its head when he grabbed its tail and slung it a third time. This time the thing flew over the round rock and landed on the far side near the cow skull. He chased after it and threw it again, and again, and again. "Yeah! Hurrah! Get him. Tear that mean old rattlesnake up," the young mice cheered from inside the cow skull.

"Hush, children!" he heard the mother mouse scold. "We live in the desert. It's a harsh place. The plants are few and far between, and in the desert everything eats everything else. That's a roadrunner. They are the quickest and best hunters of all the animals. He would just as soon eat us as the rattlesnake. Be quiet. Don't let him know we're here."

The roadrunner ignored the mice, determined to do in the rattlesnake and stay true to his word to eat the thing for supper. Trouble was, when the time came, he didn't feel like eating. His feet throbbed—clear up his strong legs and into the pit of his stomach. He hadn't noticed the sick feeling or the pain before. He was too mad. Too busy. But now . . .

Staggering, his head drooping low, he wobbled back across the open toward the creosote bush from where he'd first seen the grasshoppers. There was shade. And even though the sun was low, barely resting on the tips of the mountains to the west, he needed shade. He felt hot. Sick. The pounding in his feet was more than he could stand. He glanced down.

They were beginning to swell. Each foot had four toes—two in the front and two in the back. The snake had bitten him on the right front toe on his left foot and the left hind toe on his right foot. He must have landed with his feet almost together. The rattlesnake bit only once, but each fang sank into a different foot.

He took a few steps, then threw up. A few more steps and he threw up again. By the time he stumbled into the shade of the creosote, there was nothing left in his stomach. Not even the slightest taste of grasshopper, or scorpion, or lizard. Even the sweet flavor of the skink tail no longer lingered in his beak. He was empty. Sick. Weak.

He fell beneath the branches of the creosote bush. Resting his head on the cool sand, he lay there a moment and closed his eyes. In the darkness behind his eyelids, he could almost see his family's nest. Perched at the top of a young cholla cactus, it was a shallow, saucerlike nest made of sticks. He didn't remember being in the egg, or being born. He did remember his mother keeping him and his sister cool during the day and his father protecting them at night.

Both Mama and Daddy fed them. He remembered feeling crowded, shoved, pushed. There was always noise when his parents came with food. But when he was old enough to be truly conscious of the nest and things around it, he and his sister were alone. They haggled over food, but there was always plenty for both.

Eighteen times the sun rose, then fell behind the mountains to rest in the Great Water, before his mother and father pushed them from the nest. For the next two weeks they brought them very little food. That was because they had to learn to hunt on their own. They watched. Copied their parents. Learned.

Such a short life! What a waste. I wish they'd given me my name, he thought. *Without a name no one will remember me. Without a name, there will be nothing left but dust. Dust to be scattered by the wind and forgotten. I don't even know if I can get into the Big Desert in the Sky without a name.*

He forced his eyes to open so he could look around. Then he realized he couldn't even lift his head from the sand. This was it. He closed his eyes and waited for the end.

Chapter 3

There was a sound. A movement. Something rustling in the dry grass. He opened an eye. It was dark, dark as pitch.

I must be dead. He opened the other eye. The moon was low in the sky. A few stars twinkled above. *Are there stars and a moon in the Big Desert in the Sky?* he wondered.

Somehow he managed to raise his head. He no longer felt sick to his stomach. His legs no longer throbbed. There was a light glow to the east. It was early morning, before the sun climbed to the sky. In the distance he heard a faint, crunching sound.

He started to stand. The pain shot through his feet. It pulsed and pounded as if any second they would blow up. *I'm still alive. When you go to the*

Big Desert in the Sky, there is no pain. My feet hurt—so I've got to be alive.

The sound came closer. *A coyote. No. A coyote would come quicker.* Another crunch. Another scrape. *A bobcat. They like to sneak up on their prey, and then pounce.*

He tried to stand. Run. But he knew if he did, his feet would explode. *Just my luck. The rattlesnake didn't do me in. Now I'm going to be breakfast for some bobcat.*

He squinted, trying to see into the darkness. The sound was so close that any second he expected to see the tufted, pointy ears, the yellow cat eyes, the sharp teeth. There was nothing. The only thing he could see was a rock. It was smooth as a river stone, so slick that it shined, almost like a pool of water in the moonlight.

The rock moved. At least he thought it moved. He wasn't sure. Maybe he was imagining it. Then it moved again. Less than an inch at a time, it crept toward him. He never knew anything could move so slowly.

"Stop!" he said in the meanest clatter he could muster from deep in his throat. "You come any closer and I'll eat you."

The rock stopped. Nearer now, he could see it

better. It lay completely motionless for a while. Finally, two clawed feet and a head popped out. They didn't pop out from beneath the rock. They popped out from *inside* the rock. Right in the *middle*. Eyes wide, he leaned his head far to the side. *That can't be. Nothing lives inside a rock. Under a rock, yes. Beside a rock, yes. But not inside a rock. It just can't be! Maybe I AM dead. Either that or the poison has made me crazy.*

The head reminded him a bit of the rattlesnake. But rattlesnakes don't have feet. And there were no sharp ridges of scales over the eyes to give the head that evil look of a rattler. Then two more feet popped out from inside the back end of the rock. The head raised and two round eyes looked at him. "I thought you were dead," the head said. "Figured I'd have to shove my way under you to get to my burrow. Then after a day or so, you'd start stinking so bad I'd have to leave."

"I'm not dead yet."

"You should be. You got bit by a rattlesnake, didn't you?"

"Yes."

"Then how come you're not dead?"

"I don't know."

"Well, since you're not dead—move."

"Huh?"

"Move. So I can get in my burrow."

"Burrow? What's a burrow?"

"It's where I live. That hole where you've got your tail feathers parked. Now scoot your hind end out of the way so I can get down where it's cool and shady before the sun climbs to the sky."

The roadrunner looked one way, then stretched his neck to look the other. There was no hole. "What hole? I don't see a hole."

"You can't see it, because you're sitting on it. Move."

The strange rock was inching toward him again. He felt a chill race up his spine to his head crest. "Are you going to eat me?"

The head drew back, part way into the rock. "Good grief, NO! That's the nastiest thing I ever heard. I eat flowers and cactus and grass. Only heathens eat meat."

Cautiously the roadrunner leaned toward the strange rock. "What are you?"

The head came farther out. "I'm Berland. I'm a gopher tortoise."

"How can you live inside that rock? Isn't it heavy? Why doesn't it squash you? And how did you get in there, anyway?"

The legs drew in and the rock settled back to the ground. "I do not live inside a rock. This is my shell. It grows with me, protects me from danger and from the sun. It goes everyplace I go. It's probably not much heavier than all them feathers you're lugging around. It's part of me."

"But how can you—"

"Look, kid," Berland cut him off. "Enough with the questions! It's getting hot out here. Move your rump so I can get home. Then I'll visit all you want. Just let me inside."

"I don't know if I can."

"Try."

"But my feet hurt and I feel weak."

"Fine. I'll just tunnel under."

With that, Berland started digging. His front feet had claws. His legs were strong and flattened—just right for burrowing. Sand and gravel flew in great swoops on either side of the rock . . . er . . . shell.

The thought of those claws or strong feet whacking his sore toes forced the roadrunner to struggle to his feet. All four toes, on both feet, throbbed. They hurt something fierce. Still weak, his normally strong legs wobbled beneath him. Somehow he managed to stand and take a step. Then another.

Suddenly Berland stopped burrowing. His eyes popped wide. "Oh! My! Gosh!" In the blink of an eye, his head and feet disappeared inside his shell.

The roadrunner frowned down at the tortoise. "What is it? What's wrong?"

"Ah . . . er . . . nothing." The muffled sound of Berland's stammering came from inside his shell. "It's just . . . well . . . never mind."

"Go on," the roadrunner urged. "I don't know how much longer I can stand here."

Berland waddled behind him. The last thing he saw was the hind legs and a tiny tail disappear into a hole in the ground. If he could just get his feet to move—just take another step or two—he could turn and look at the hole while they talked.

Suddenly a familiar cooing sound caught his ear. He glanced toward the noise. It was Mama and Daddy. "There he is, Lithe! We found him."

Fast as the wind, both rushed toward him. "Where have you been?" Mama scolded with an angry tone. "Young man—you are in *so much* trouble."

"Yesterday was to be your Naming," Daddy clattered as he raced along beside her. "You've been gone all night. You were supposed to . . ."

Both birds slid to a stop, looking down at their son. Four eyes flashed wide. Their head crests sprang up so straight they almost touched the other's long beak.

"Oh! My! Gosh!"

Chapter 4

Mama and Daddy agreed that the swelling would go down in a day or two. Even Berland—although he was hard to understand, since his voice came from so deep in the ground—agreed. "Don't sweat it, kid," the muffled voice seemed to echo. "You'll be back to normal in no time."

When the young roadrunner had first glanced down to see why everyone was screeching "Oh! My! Gosh!" he felt like throwing up. But since his stomach was empty, all he could do was gag and gasp. He sank to the ground and covered the ghastly-looking things with his feathers. Hiding them, not only from his mother and father, but from his own eyes as well.

His once strong, handsome feet looked horrible. They were more than three times bigger than they were supposed to be. They were as round and bulbous as he imagined the limbs of the giant saguaro cactus his father had told him about.

"Perhaps we could help," Mama suggested.

"Yesterday was The Naming," Daddy said. "The girl was there. Her name shall forever be Sprite of the Foote Clan. The boy was not there for The Naming. It is past time and too late."

Mama puffed out her feathers. "But he doesn't have his name. It's not too late until he has his name."

"Remember the Rule of Nature, Lithe. We cannot break the Rule!"

There was much talk. Much discussion. They ran a ways to speak in private. Not understanding, and worried, the young roadrunner glanced at the dark hole beside him. "Berland? Berland, you still in there?"

"I'm here, kid."

"Why do Mama and Daddy have to go talk about the Rule? What rule? If they made the Rule, why can't they break it?"

"The Rule is not your mother's or father's. It's not even a roadrunner rule. The rule is of Nature itself. For hundreds of years, Nature's rule of the desert has been unchanged—survive. Only the strong can do this. To break this rule—to tamper with it or change it—could mean disaster."

"I don't get it."

A scraping sound came from inside the dark hole. There was movement, crawling. When Berland spoke again, his voice seemed a little louder, clearer.

"Let's take you, for instance. With roadrunners, your mother and father fed you when you were little, right?"

"Well . . . me and my sister—right."

"They brought every bite of food to you. You didn't do anything but sit in your nest and squawk. Then you were fledged."

"Fledged?"

"They shoved you out of the nest."

With a sigh, the roadrunner felt his long tail twitch. "I remember that, too."

"Didn't like it, either, did you?"

"No."

There was more scratching and scraping from inside the hole. "You probably squawked and yelled when they didn't bring food. But you watched them. Saw how they did things. Until finally you figured you could try it yourself."

Nodding, the roadrunner preened his wing feathers with his long beak. "I wasn't very good at it," he admitted.

"Not at first," Berland said, chuckling. "So they helped out a little. But after a while you got better. They didn't help as much. Hardly brought you anything to eat. You did it for yourself. Up until you had that run in with that baby rattler, I bet you were catching almost everything—all by yourself."

The roadrunner felt his chest puff out. "I was doing great! Grasshoppers, lizards, almost had a skink, but his tail broke off, and . . ."

"And," Berland helped him out, "then you got bit. You're weak and hurt and your feet are swollen up something terrible. It was your time. Your time to be on your own. Your time to explore. Your time to meet others of your kind. Your time to grow, mature, find your own territory.

"Nature said it is your time. You can no longer go back to your nest. You can no longer depend on your parents for help and food. But, now—since you're weak and hurt—you need help. Your mother and father are concerned that if they help, they will break the Rule. But they're not sure. That's why they're having such a tough time deciding."

There was more scraping and scratching. The

roadrunner tilted his head to the side. Berland's head appeared. In the shadows, he could see the front of the tortoise's shell and his two front feet. "You said if they break the Rule of Nature it would be a disaster. Is that a bad thing?"

Berland nodded. "Very bad. The desert does not forgive mistakes or breaking the Rule. As you grow, it takes more and more food to fill you up. More and more food to help you grow big and strong. You roadrunners are the best hunters in the desert. Even so, food is hard to find. No matter how much they love you, or how much they care for you, your mother and father know that if they continue to feed you, there won't be enough food for the three of you.

"You will not grow. You will become weaker and weaker. By sharing their food, your parents won't have enough to keep their strength up, either. They'll become weaker and weaker, too. The time of the Cold is growing near. The time when the bugs and lizards and even the snakes you feed on will become harder to find. If you're not strong or ready, all three of you will either starve or become easy prey for a bobcat or coyote. To what clan do you belong?"

"We are the Foote Clan."

"If you and your parents are gone, your sister . . . ah . . . er . . . what was her name?"

"Sprite."

"Yeah, Sprite. She will be the only one left. If something happens to her, there will be no more of your Clan. If she survives, finds a mate, and has a family, and then breaks the Rule of Nature, not only the Foote Clan, but another clan as well, may be gone. Nature does not forgive. To break the Rule could mean the end of the roadrunners. Forever."

Laying his head against the sand, the roadrunner thought about what Berland said. He felt very scared and a little ashamed.

"Now do you see why their decision is so hard?" the tortoise asked. "Why they must know—for sure—that they are doing the right thing?"

His beak scratched the sand when he nodded his head. When his mother and father returned, Berland was at the very top of his burrow. They nodded to him, then turned their attention to their son. "The decision is made," his father began. "Only the strong survive."

The young bird felt his heart sink clear to the very bottom of his throbbing, aching, enormous feet.

Chapter 5

"You are strong!" Daddy continued, much to the young bird's surprise. "If you were not strong, you would not have survived the bite of the rattlesnake. The time of The Naming has come. BUT—you do not have your name. There is enough food nearby for two sunrises. We will help you. This will not break the Rule.

"When the sun climbs to the sky for the third time—no matter what—you will be given your name. After that, your mother and I will be with you no more."

For two days the roadrunner's parents brought him mice, lizards, grasshoppers, and a skink (which no longer had its tail). The second day, his father even brought a huge collared lizard that was almost too big for the young bird to swallow. Mama brought a gopher snake the same day.

During the time when the sun was high in the sky, they rested, always watchful. Then they hunted again. At night Mama went a few yards from the bush in one direction and Daddy went in the other. If a bobcat or coyote came, they would make it chase them so their son would be safe.

With each bite, with each morsel of food, the young roadrunner felt stronger. Braver. The first day, his feet still ached and throbbed. He forced himself to stand and take a few steps. The second day, he walked around. Watchful, careful, he left the safety of the creosote bush. The pain was not so bad anymore. It was still hard to walk, but he could do it. Just before the sun climbed to the sky on the third day, he ran to the old cow skull and back. It didn't hurt much at all, and he stumbled and tripped only a couple of times.

Just as the sun peeked above the mountains to the east, Mama and Daddy raced across the sand toward him. Mama leaned forward and handed him a small horned lizard. He gobbled it down. Daddy shot her a look but didn't say anything. Ruffling his feathers, he stood tall and straight. "It is the time of The Naming, my son. There is a fat, juicy, grasshopper on a weed beneath that mesquite tree," he said, pointing his beak at the ridge. "When the very bottom of the sun rests on the crest of the mountain, you will stand. Race over and catch the grasshopper, then race back. As is custom, we shall watch. Observe your speed, agility, and alertness. When you return, a name will be given."

It was an exciting time. He felt the muscles tense in his legs as he watched the sun inch higher. *Almost there. Any second now. Wait for it!* Even Berland poked his head from his burrow to watch the ceremony.

For only an instant, the very bottom of the sun rested on the sharp peak of the mountain. The young roadrunner leaped to his feet. "Whoops!" he heard Berland shriek from beside him. When he glanced down, Berland's head quickly drew back into his shell.

When Mama glanced down, her mouth fell open. Her eyes grew big around as the moon. Daddy's feathers bristled, then smoothed down as his wings drooped. He forced his head crest high and cleared his throat. "Go! Your name will be waiting for you when you return."

The young roadrunner raced off. Only he didn't

seem to move as fast as he had a couple of days ago. His feet didn't hurt, but they felt heavy. A *thud* and *thump* sound raced with him across the sand. He tripped once but kept his balance. The grasshopper jumped from the mesquite. He leaped to catch it in flight. Although the leap wasn't nearly as high as he planned, he still managed to grab the thing with the very tip of his sharp beak.

He landed on some dried twigs. There was a loud *crack*. The sound was a little strange, but he didn't take the time to think about it or even look down. Instantly, grasshopper in beak, he spun and raced back to his parents. Proudly, he showed it to them, then swallowed it down. Both tried to smile, but their smiles weren't very convincing. They both tried to stand tall and proud, but Mama's wings drooped, and Daddy's head crest was flat. Finally, they looked at each other, nodded, then turned to him. "From this day forward," they spoke together, "you shall be known as . . ."

Chapter 6

"Move."

He heard the voice, but all he could do was sit and sulk. "Move!"

"No!"

Something nudged the right hind toe of his left foot. He didn't budge. "MOVE!!!"

"No."

There was a long silence before Berland's muffled voice came again. "Your feet still hurt?"

"Huh?"

"Do your feet still hurt?"

"No."

He felt the breath on his toe when the old tortoise sighed. "Good. Then you won't mind if I just take a bite out of this one that's blocking my burrow."

He waited a moment, and when there was no

response from the bird he sighed again. "Okay. I'm gonna count to three. You don't move this toe out of my way, I'm gonna bite it. One . . . two . . ."

The roadrunner hopped to his feet and stepped aside.

"About time," Berland muttered as he crawled out into the late afternoon sun.

The bird glared down at him. Berland stretched his legs and lifted his shell clear off the ground. It made him look taller. Bigger. Then he slowly shook his head and sank back down. "I have lived in this desert for seventy-five seasons. I survived the crows and you roadrunners my first two seasons, when I was small and my shell was delicate. I survived the coyotes, and the droughts, and the three times I got flipped on my back for courting a girl who already had a bigger, stronger boyfriend.

"In my heyday, my shell had nice, hard, sharp ridges. Now it's worn smooth as a wet rock in the arroyo, with age. I've seen a lot. I've done a lot. But in all my years, I have *never*—and I do mean NEVER—met a bird as stubborn, bullheaded, and ungrateful as you."

The bird just glared down at him. "First off, you survive the rattlesnake. And it wasn't because you were strong. It was just dumb luck! Molly told me about it when I was walking toward my burrow, that first night we met."

"Who's Molly?"

"Molly Mouse," Berland explained. "You know. She and her kids live in the cow skull. She said the thing bit two of her children. The snake used up most of its venom to catch food. When you landed on it, all it had left was half a drop or so at the tip of each fang. Any more than that, and you would have been buzzard bait.

"Then . . . your parents loved you so much they were willing to risk breaking the Rule of Nature, just to help you out. Two days they spent bringing you every morsel of food they could find. Helped you recover. Kept you alive."

The roadrunner ruffled his feathers. Jaw muscles clamped his beak so tight he could hear the grinding sound inside his head. "But they lied to me. So did *you.*"

Berland blinked. "Nobody lied to you, you ungrateful little snot. We thought the swelling *would* go down. And it did. Your feet aren't nearly as big as they were."

"They're still twice as big as they're supposed to be. They're big as Mama's and Daddy's feet put together. They're so big and heavy, when I run it sounds like . . . like . . ."

His voice trailing off in surrender, he sank to the ground and ruffled into the sand.

"Like thunder," Berland finished what he was trying to say. "Got to admit, kid. When I first saw those feet of yours, it startled me. I really did think the swelling would be gone. Then this morning, at the time of The Naming, I kind of backed down into my burrow and . . . well . . . when you took off, the sound of those feet pounding on the ground *did* remind me of . . . it did sound a bit like . . ."

"Thunder!" The roadrunner snarled. He ruffled his feathers. "Thunder of the Foote Clan! It's a horrible name. I wanted a name like Speedy, or Lite, or . . . or Hunter . . . or . . ."

"Thunder is just a name, kid. You don't get to pick your name. Your parents don't even get to pick. Your name has to be what you are—who you are. Thunder is the only thing they *could* have named you."

Thunder raised up and peeked beneath his feathers at his feet. "They're not only fatter, but longer, too. I keep tripping over them. It's hard to hunt. And if a coyote . . ." His voice trailing off once more, he sank back to the ground.

"It'll just take some getting used to, kid. You'll learn. Give it a while. The more you run, the stronger your legs will be. You'll get used to your feet, too. Quit stumbling over twigs and rocks. The more you fly, the stronger your wings will be. In no time at all—"

"But it's too hard!" Thunder whined, cutting Berland off. "I can't do it!"

The old tortoise glared up at him. Then with a sigh, he moved on his way. "Nobody ever told you life was gonna be easy," he said as he walked. "If anybody does, they're lying to you. Life's never easy. Life is hard."

Thunder wanted to ask if he was leaving, but it was plain to see that he was. He wanted to ask if he was going back to his burrow. He didn't. He didn't want to talk to the tortoise anymore. He was too mad and too discouraged. So he just sat in the sand as Berland inched away.

The evening sun cast a long shadow from the creosote bush. Just beyond the shade, Berland stopped and looked back over his shoulder. "Maybe I'll see you around, kid," he called. "That is *if* you get off your lazy tail feathers and do something. You know, like hunt, or run, or practice flying.

"'Course, you keep sitting there, feeling sorry for

yourself, I'll see you in about a month or so. When I come back this way. Well . . . I won't really see you. I'll just see what's left of your lazy carcass after the buzzards and the fire ants are through with it."

With that he turned and waddled on his way. Thunder felt his round eyes tighten to tiny slits. His head crest arched high. *LAZY??! He told me to get off my LAZY tail feathers? He said there'd be nothing left but my LAZY carcass? That's not a nice thing to say. I thought Berland was my friend. Even he's left me. Some friend. A real friend would never call another friend lazy. It's not fair. It's not right for him to say things like that!*

All night he lay there thinking about what Berland had called him. He brooded about it, hearing the words over and over again in his head.

Brooding is a bad thing. Spending the whole night awake and puffed up about something another says is a big waste of time. But for Thunder . . . the more Thunder brooded, the madder he got.

Chapter 1

The tip of the sun had not yet peeked above the mountains when the sound of thunder echoed across the desert. Okay . . . well . . . it wasn't *that* bad. But to Thunder, it was. Each time his big feet hit the ground, he could hear the *thud*! It seemed to drum inside his head like the roar of a spring storm.

When there had been enough light to see, he'd remembered. "Look before you leap." There was no movement between the creosote bush and the first ridge to the east. He stood, stretched for only a second, and glared down at the empty burrow beside him. "Teach you to call me lazy," he muttered. Then he raced to the ridge.

Each step felt heavy. His big feet felt thick, swollen, and hard to lift. Still, he ran just fine.

Maybe not as fast as he used to, but just fine. With each step, there was a loud *thump* when his feet struck the ground.

At the top of the ridge, he took a quick peek to see if he could find Berland. Far to his left, near some rocks, there were five kangaroo rats kicking sand at a sidewinder. Outnumbered and blinded by the flying, stinging sand, the snake retreated and left the rats' nest area.

Two collared lizards, bright green with black bands around their necks, were doing push-ups on some boulders, far to the right. Thunder guessed they were trying to impress the plainer-looking, speckled, brown female who watched. There was no Berland.

Thunder sprinted back to the creosote bush. Without even slowing to catch his breath, he spun and raced to the ridge again. Four times. Back and forth. Back and forth. Back and . . .

The irritating, thudding, thumping, thundering sound went with him each time he ran. But already his legs felt stronger. In all four trips to the ridge, he never stumbled. Not even once. Glaring down at the empty burrow beside him, he sat beneath the creosote bush to catch his breath. "I'll show you," he muttered again.

Berland had a head start. The whole night in fact. But as slow as the old tortoise moved, he'd catch him in no time. When he found Berland, he'd tell him what a rotten friend he really was. He'd let him know, in no uncertain terms, that he no longer was—and never would be—friends with any tortoise. He was so mad he might even use his beak to flip the stupid tortoise over onto his back. That would scare him. Teach him a lesson. Then— well, he wasn't *that* mad. He'd probably tip him upright before he left.

Trotting this time instead of sprinting, his feet didn't make quite as much noise as they pounded the desert sand. At the top of the ridge, he paused to take a good look before he continued on Berland's trail.

The two collared lizards were still doing their push-ups. The female egged them on with her own head bobs and nods. To the east, the kangaroo rats had driven off the sidewinder. They were busy gobbling prickly pear flowers, trying to fill their tummies before the sun drove them to the safety of their burrows. Between the lizards and the kangaroo rats, there was no motion except for grasshoppers and . . .

No, wait! Something . . . back to the north.

Sharp eyes focused. *Just the kangaroo rats,* Thunder decided. No! There was something more. A movement . . . only he couldn't quite tell . . .

A tuft of hair, not more than twelve to fifteen tiny strands that bunched together and rose to a sharp point. They wiggled, but only slightly, in the breeze. A sharp pointed ear. A second ear. A head—rising from behind a sagebrush so slowly it was almost like watching Berland walk. The head rose higher. Higher.

Bobcat!

The breath stopped in Thunder's throat. He didn't move. Didn't blink. Sure the yellow eyes were not on him, he quickly scanned the desert. Nothing else—only one bobcat. Less than an inch at a time, it moved toward the kangaroo rats. All their hopping around and sand kicking had driven off the sidewinder. But the commotion had attracted an even more deadly hunter.

When the bobcat sprang, it almost made Thunder jump. The kangaroo rats sprang, too. Their strong back legs thrust them into the air. Tails spinning to keep their balance, they hopped again the instant their legs touched the sand, this time in a different direction.

The bobcat landed on empty sand. It swatted

with a paw. The kangaroo rat was gone. The bobcat reached out the other paw. That kangaroo rat escaped, too, the bobcat's claws just barely missing the tip of its long, black-tipped tail. Rats ran and hopped in every direction. The cat pounced and swatted in every direction. When the dust finally cleared, all five kangaroo rats had made it back to the safety of their burrows, and the bobcat sat panting. Looking quite unconcerned, it sat down on its little stub tail, licked the top of its paws, and started cleaning its whiskers—as if it couldn't care less.

Thunder knew if he left the ridge, the bobcat would see the movement. He also knew that coyotes could run and trot for miles without getting tired, but bobcats were sprinters. Much quicker than coyotes, they could run only short distances. If he went to the right, away from the kangaroo rat burrows, the bobcat would see him. It would realize, however, that it could never catch a roadrunner. Not at this distance.

Thunder darted toward the collared lizards. At the rock outcropping, he stopped to check on the bobcat. It was still washing its whiskers. Suddenly there was a high, shrill clicking sound from beside him.

"Earthquake!"

The brown, speckled girl lizard slipped to a crevice between two boulders. The smaller of the male collared lizards stopped doing his push-ups. Eyes big and scared, he echoed the girl lizard's clicks. "Earthquake. Run for your life!"

The other male didn't run, though. Mouth gaping wide, he stood on the rock and looked down at Thunder. Then he started laughing. "That wasn't an earthquake," he said, chuckling. "You guys need to come look at this bird. He's got the biggest feet I ever saw. They're huge! This is hilarious."

Then he laughed and laughed and laughed, until Thunder thought he was going to fall off the rock.

Chapter 8

When the desert sun rose high and the day grew so hot that the sand seemed to wave and ripple as if it were alive, Thunder found shade beneath some mesquite trees at the edge of a wide canyon. The day before, except for the horned lizard his mother had given him, he had eaten nothing. He'd been too busy pouting and feeling sorry for himself. But now, there was no need to hunt until the sun started down and it was cooler.

That was because the big, male, collared lizard had been quite satisfying. Satisfying—not only because he was so big he'd filled Thunder's tummy better than a whole field of grasshoppers, but because it had shut up his laughter.

As he rested in the shade, Thunder watched the wide canyon. There were no predators. No Berland.

In the evening he crossed the canyon. There were plenty of grasshoppers and a few cicadas. Those were easy to find, especially when they came from their cocoons. They stretched and fluttered their wings to dry them so they could fly. All Thunder had to do was watch for the movement.

Before nightfall, he found a high ridge where he could see in all directions. Maybe Berland was holed up in the shade someplace. During the cool part at the end of the day, he would probably be on the move again and Thunder would spot him. Then again, maybe he had already passed the old tortoise.

The next day, as he moved farther toward the rising sun, the land began to change. There was less sand, more short grass, mesquite, and sagebrush. When the day grew hot he rested in the shade at the edge of a huge thicket. Red berries dangled from the branches of the short bushes. Toward the center of the thicket, the brush was so dense he could hardly see through it.

It was a good place to rest . . . until he spotted the coyotes. There were two. They came from the south, trotting at an easy but steady lope. They were still a good ways off and hadn't spotted him.

So he decided it would be safer to move farther into the thicket.

A mouse must have scampered into some dry grass in their path. Both coyotes stopped, listened, then pounced. When their heads were down and their noses sniffing the grass, Thunder eased to his feet. He glanced one last time to make sure they were still busy trying to figure out where the mouse went, then darted into the thicket.

Running through heavy brush was different from running on the open desert sand. Mama and Daddy had told him and his sister this. One day, they had taken them to the arroyo. Since water flowed from the flats and streamed into the low places, many plants grew there. Instead of being sparse and spread out, shrubs and bushes were close together.

While Mama and Daddy watched for predators, he and his sister had practiced racing through the brush. He'd figured out that if he kept his wings tight against his side and ran crouched close to the ground, it was easier. It helped when ducking the low limbs. Of course, he had to hop over the limbs that were too low to duck, and dodge around others.

No problem. Roadrunners are so quick and agile they can dart through heavy brush faster than most coyotes can sprint across the open sand. Trouble was . . . Thunder's big feet caught on everything. He tripped over limbs. Twigs cracked beneath his toes. He stumbled. Crashed into a fork of one branch, and had to back up to pull his neck loose. He ran harder. Staying clear of one trunk, he stubbed his toe on another. Tripped and slid on his chin. Clambering to his feet, he caught his toe on a root that sent him sprawling on his beak.

When he pulled it from the ground, he spit dirt for the next twenty yards. There was so much racket he couldn't even hear his feet thundering on the ground. A little over midway through the thicket, he stopped and looked back.

Sure enough, the coyotes had heard the ruckus. Thunder saw them trotting toward his thicket. Heads up and ears perked, they didn't move at a leisurely trot. They were coming quick—suspecting from the noise that there were at least twenty to thirty rabbits or something, just waiting to be their dinner.

Once clear of the horrible, tangled, treacherous thicket, Thunder stopped by a plum patch. His sharp eyes spotted the coyotes on the opposite side. They listened. Waited. When there was no sound, one started in while the other circled to the right.

Thunder sprinted from the plums to the left so the thick brush between them would help hide his escape. There was another plum patch about a hundred yards away. He made for that but didn't even think about going into it. Instead he circled, still trying to stay out of sight of the two coyotes.

It worked. Once past the plum patch, he found a small ridge. Crouching low, he ducked behind it and ran—but not as far as he wanted to. Struggling and fighting his way through the brush had been tougher than he thought. That and the hot sun that beat down, almost straight overhead, were almost enough to do him in. He stopped at the edge of the little ridge. Beak wide open and tongue dangling out, he gasped for air.

Coyotes don't hunt during the heat of the day, he thought. *They rest in the shade like we do. What's wrong with these guys?* Easing to where he could stretch his neck to see over the crest of the little ridge, he sighted the two coyotes.

They were already at the second plum patch. Noses popping and close to the ground, they were trailing him, following a path around the plum patch, the same way he had gone. Panting, sucking the hot air as hard and fast as he could, Thunder could only hope he had enough energy and speed left to outrun them if they . . .

Suddenly they stopped. Ears perked. Two heads snapped toward the plum thicket. A movement from inside the brush caught Thunder's eye. The cover was so thick he couldn't tell what it was.

The coyotes must have seen the movement, too. They raced into the thicket, crashing and crunching as their charge snapped limbs and twigs. The two of them were making almost as much noise as he had made with his big feet.

Whatever was there waited until they were well inside the plum thicket. Then it burst from the other side. Thunder's eyes flashed wide. It was a roadrunner. Not Mama or Daddy—this roadrunner was young, like him. It was . . . it was . . .

Thunder's heart leaped up in his throat. He held his breath. His eyes flashed wide in horror. Then he blinked.

Chapter 9

Then he blinked again. No! It wasn't Sprite, either. It was a girl bird, all right. She was small and quick, like his sister. Only it wasn't his sister.

The bird let the two coyotes get almost to the middle of the thicket before she shot out the other side. She ducked behind the little ridge where Thunder had gone, only in the opposite direction. When he saw her again, she popped over the ridge on the far side of the first thicket, where he'd almost gotten stuck. Without even slowing down, she scampered right for the center of the thick, tangled brush.

To Thunder's surprise, she didn't stay there and wait. Instead she ran right through the middle of the thicket, came out, and ran back to the plum patch where the coyotes had first seen her.

What she did next surprised him even more. At the center of the plum patch, she fluttered and hopped to the very top of the tallest bush. The coyotes were behind the ridge, so they couldn't see her. She paused for only a second to catch her breath, then flew.

Roadrunners don't fly very well or very far. She barely cleared the near side of the thicket when her underside started scraping branches. She fluttered to the ground and sprinted over the ridge.

For a moment or two, he lost sight of her. The coyotes appeared beside the first plum patch. One circled around to the far side of the brush. There it sat and waited. The other crashed straight for the middle, following the girl roadrunner's trail. Another movement caught Thunder's eye. Crouched low behind his ridge, he saw the girl roadrunner race straight toward him. Quickly he squatted and ruffled his feathers to hide his hideous feet. She darted past, less than a foot from where he sat. She didn't even look at him when she snipped, "Thanks a lot, dork!"

Thunder's mouth fell open.

"Huh?"

She was moving so fast it took her a few yards to stop. She turned to glare at him. "I was sitting there, minding my own business, when you come crashing through that other plum patch. Made so much noise, every coyote in the country probably heard you. Then you run right past where I'm resting and bring those two right to me. Thanks a lot!"

She turned and took off again. When she glanced back over her shoulder and saw he was still sitting there, she stopped again. "What are you waiting for?"

"Huh?"

Her mouth arched on one side behind her beak. Sneering at him, she wobbled her head back and forth. "You hard of hearing? Or is 'Huh' the only word you know?" She pointed her beak toward the thicket on the other side of the ridge. "Coyotes are slow and dumb—but they're not totally stupid. Sooner or later, they're going to find one of our trails. Figure out where we went. Now quit sitting there waiting for them. Get up. We need to get out of here before they come."

Thunder started to stand, then hesitated. The girl was already on the move. "We'll run a crisscross for about a mile," she instructed. "They usually don't follow more than that. And the crisscross always confuses them, anyway. Then we'll track single file for a ways, just to be on the safe side."

He knew the crisscross. It was a running pattern Mama and Daddy had taught Sprite and him when they were just out of the nest. A way to confuse coyotes and get them off your tail feathers. Since the girl was ahead of him and not looking back, he hopped to his feet.

When she'd raced toward him behind the ridge, she'd come straight as a yucca leaf. Now there were two of them. She ran to the left. Thunder ran in the same direction, then swung to the right. After a ways, just before she reached the top of the little ridge where the coyotes might see her, she turned right. At the same time, Thunder turned left. Their trails crossed. When he reached the crest of the little ridge, he turned toward her—crossing their trails again and again.

After a mile or so, she made a cooing sound in her throat. This time when she crossed in front of him, Thunder followed her. He even ran, placing his feet in her exact tracks.

Well . . . he tried to step in her tracks. As he glanced back, the footprints he left were so big he couldn't see her tracks at all.

Running in the hot desert sun is downright dumb. All animals know that—especially roadrunners. Problem was, they had to travel farther than they planned because they couldn't find shade or a place where they could watch for the coyotes.

They finally climbed a high knoll. There were some big boulders at the crest that offered shade. Thunder dropped his feathers over his feet the second he reached the knoll. The girl turned, found a spot where she could watch the other way, then she sat, too.

Tongues dangling and beaks open wide, gasping for air, both were so tired and exhausted they sat for a long time without a word. Finally, when their body temperatures had cooled and they could breathe, she said, "I am Agile'eka of the Swift Clan. We come from the east, near the rising sun."

She sat, patiently waiting. When Thunder didn't introduce himself, she gave a little snort. "My name is Agile'eka. What's your name?"

Trying to ignore her, Thunder scanned the west for any movement. The sun was straight overhead. The wind didn't blow. Everything was still. "What's your name?" she clattered, louder this time.

"Thunder of the Foote Clan."

"That name fits you," she scoffed.

Thunder tilted his head to the side. "Just exactly what do you mean by that?"

"I mean, as much racket as you made in that

plum patch, it's little wonder they named you Thunder."

"It wasn't my fault."

"What do you mean, it wasn't your fault? Those two coyotes didn't make as much noise as you did. Didn't your parents ever teach you how to be quiet when you're running through brush?"

Thunder felt his head crest bristle. "My parents taught me very well. Fact is, up until about three or four days ago, I bet I could have gone through that thicket quieter and quicker than you did."

"So what happened three days ago?"

"Nothing."

He stuck his beak in the air and gazed back at the desert.

"Nothing? Then why did you say up until about three days ago you could have run through the plums quieter and quicker than me? What happened?"

"Nothing!"

"You're just making it up, aren't you? You're just noisy. You're just making up excuses for being such a klutz."

"Am not."

"Are too."

"Am not!"

"Yeah, right."

Thunder was ashamed and embarrassed. At the same time, he was getting mad! She didn't even know him, yet she was calling him a liar. *I'll show her*, he thought. *I'll teach her to call me a liar!* With that, he eased up. Agile'eka's eyes popped wide.

"Oh! My! Gosh!"

Chapter 10

When Agile'eka's eyes flashed wide, Thunder didn't sink down and nestle his feathers over his feet. He dropped like a rock.

Any second, he expected her to say something smart, like, "I thought I heard thunder when we were running. Guess it was just those big, fat feet of yours." Or even worse, she might start laughing like the collared lizards had. Instead she dropped her watchful gaze from the horizon and looked him straight in the eye.

"How did it happen?"

"Rattlesnake," Thunder answered.

Her feathers rippled as if grabbed by a chill. Then she turned her attention back to the coyotes. Braced and ready, Thunder waited. Any second now, she was going to say something. Any second she'd burst out giggling. He waited, and waited, and waited. He felt his head crest bristle. "Aren't you gonna laugh at my feet?"

She glanced at the ground, not looking at him. "There's nothing funny about a rattlesnake," she said with a sigh. "When we were fledged, there were three of us. My two brothers and myself. Near The Naming time our father took us to the cliffs beyond the big tree forest. He found a diamond-back rattlesnake and—"

She broke off and quietly flattened closer to the ground. "There they are!"

Since Thunder was watching the opposite direction, he had to turn his head slightly. The two coyotes topped the little ridge, far in the distance. About ten yards apart, they followed the trails of the two roadrunners with their noses. Not watching where they were going, and trotting fast when the two paths merged together, they bumped into each other. There was considerable snarling and snapping. When they put their noses to the ground again, they couldn't decide which way to go. Moving side by side, they circled one way, then the other. Then, still growling and fussing at each other, they trotted back the way they had come.

"What happened with the rattlesnake?" Thunder asked. "Did it get your father?"

Agile'eka shuddered. "No. We all watched and Daddy showed us how it was done. He warned us to wait until we were grown before we tried to catch a snake. He told us to be sure the snake was not too big or too strong. And . . . and . . ."

"And?" Thunder urged.

"And . . . well," she stammered. "I was named Agile'eka because I was nimble and agile. My younger brother was Zipp. My older brother was Dash, because he was always the fastest. The strongest. He ran like the wind. Not just to hunt for food or to escape, he ran just to run. He loved to run." There was a strange, sad clicking sound from her throat when she swallowed. "The very next day, after The Naming, we left our home to strike out on our own. The three of us stayed close in the morning. During the high sun, we rested in the shade together. When it cooled we each went our own way.

"I stopped on a high hill where I could spot grasshoppers or mice. Instead I saw Dash. He was hopping and dodging, lifting one wing at a time. From watching Daddy I knew he was trying to get a snake to strike. But when it finally did, I couldn't believe my eyes.

"The thing was enormous. Even as far away as I was, I could see the sharp, devil horns above his eyes. When it opened its mouth to strike, the fangs were as long as my toes. The thing was longer than Dash. Thick and big around as a cactus.

"I raced down the hill to tell Dash to stop—to warn him that the snake was too big. From the corner of my eye, I could see Zipp racing toward him, too. We were too late. Dash grabbed the thing by the tail and yanked. The snake was too big. Too strong. Instead of straightening so Dash could throw him against the rocks, he was still half coiled. And he . . . he . . ."

"The coyotes are back!" Thunder had seen the coyotes at the top of the ridge some thirty seconds earlier. He knew Agile'eka had probably seen them, too. But she was having so much trouble telling about her brother—the sadness of her voice was so painful—that he told her about the coyotes so she wouldn't have to finish her story.

"You think we should move?" she asked.

Confused, the coyotes sniffed around a moment. Then, having lost the scent, they headed to the northeast. The wrong direction. Even so, Thunder eased to his feet.

"We probably need to move on," he answered.

They found shade beneath an old prickly pear. The plant was so ancient, and the pod branches so high, it gave as much shade as a mesquite. Careful not to say anything about her brother or rattlesnakes, Thunder asked her about the big tree forest that she'd mentioned when they first met.

He had always wanted to see where the sun rose in the east. But when she described all the trees and branches and brush, he remembered the trouble he'd had running through the plum patch. She told about plenty of water. It was held in ponds and streams—even rivers with high trees along the banks. It sounded interesting, but Thunder realized east was not the way for him to go.

She also told of farms and strange enormous animals called cows. When he told her he had seen cows and knew what they were, she told him they were not nearly as strange as people animals. Those he had not heard of. She told him how they moved on two legs, slow and clumsy, but how they also had machines that roared and streaked across the plains faster than the fastest roadrunner. Her description of the strange creatures was downright frightening.

She asked him about the west, where he had come from. She told him it was a place *she* had always wanted to see. He described the cholla and the creosote bushes and the saltbush.

She never mentioned his feet, but she did want to know how he could have survived a rattlesnake bite. He told her what Berland had heard from Molly Mouse about how the young rattler had bitten two of her children and had only a tiny bit of venom left in its fangs when it bit him.

When she asked who Berland was, Thunder—careful not to mention the snake again—described the gopher tortoise and explained how they met. He also told her how he'd thought Berland was his friend until he started calling him names. And how when he caught up with him, he was going to flip him over on his back and threaten to leave him for the buzzards.

When it cooled, they followed the sun. They found scorpions and a couple of lizards for supper. When dark came, they nestled down at the crest of a high ridge. They weren't girlfriend and boyfriend, or anything like that. But it was easier to watch when there were two instead of just one. Besides, being alone . . . well . . . being alone is kind of . . . lonely.

Chapter 11

Thunder had never seen rain. Mama and Daddy had told them about it, but all he could do was imagine. It was hard to do. He simply couldn't understand how water could come from the sky. It belonged on the ground, like the pool in the deep part of the arroyo, about a mile or so from where he was born.

The farther southwest he and Agile'eka moved, the harder it was to find any water. With no rain and the hot desert sun, even the barrel cactus were beginning to shrivel. Instead of seeking the safety of the high ground, the two roadrunners stayed to the arroyos and dry washes. For three days they went without a drink. The grasshoppers provided enough moisture—but just barely.

The evening of the fourth day, they came to a place where the arroyo widened. The steep, rock-cluttered walls fell back, making a wide, flat area. Gnarled and twisted, cottonwood trees speckled a path down the center where a stream had once run. Over a mile away, the steep walls of the canyon seemed to close. There were tall, green plants growing in the streambed. Their leaves long and pointed like the yucca, they grew thick and close together. But as he stood watching the valley, he noticed something else.

The floor of the wide arroyo seemed alive. There was movement as far as his eye could see, as if the ground were wriggling and crawling. His head crest rose. Lips behind his beak curled to a smile. "Tarantulas," he whispered.

Thunder's mother had told him that sometimes there were hundreds upon hundreds of tarantulas born from one hatch. Although these tarantulas were two to three weeks old, and no longer babies, the hatch must have been plentiful. They seemed to be everywhere.

Agile'eka was a little nervous at first. The tarantulas would rock back on their hind legs, raising their front pair as if to fight. Their jawlike chelicera and fangs snapped dangerously. "They're just trying to scare you," Thunder assured her.

"But what if they bite me?"

"They can't hurt you. Even the grown ones can't bite through our beak or feathers." Quick as a wink he grabbed one and swallowed. "See?"

"I don't know."

He grabbed another, tossed it, and snatched it out of the air while it was still spinning. "If you're still scared, stab them with your beak first. Then eat them."

They filled their tummies. Even when night fell, a few tarantulas strolled by where they rested on the high ground. With all this juicy food about, the roadrunners didn't even think about water.

All roadrunners must find their own place in the world. Their own territory. *Maybe this is our territory. Mine and Agile'eka's,* Thunder thought. *The valley is wide and long. There's more than enough food for a whole family of roadrunners. There might even be some water at the far end, where all the trees are so thick. Tomorrow I'll find out.*

That evening, they talked. She liked the valley, too. They were both too young to start a family. Now was the time to explore and learn and see the world. "But," she said, smiling, "maybe in a year or so we could meet here. Who knows?"

When morning came and they set out to see if there was water at the far end of the valley, they found more than they counted on. Thunder moved down one side of the valley and Agile'eka made her way down the other. There was no rush. Always watchful, but at a leisurely pace, they ate as they went toward the place where the valley narrowed.

Thunder smelled water long before he saw it. The sand was flat and smooth. Tall blades of grass sprang up, so thick he couldn't see through them. The leaves were shaped like the yucca, but not hard and stiff. These leaves were so tender and limber they swayed with the gentle breeze. Strange flowers grew at the end of long stalks. They were brown and round like a stick of wood, but kind of fuzzy looking.

As the smell of water became stronger, the brush and grass and trees grew so thick he couldn't see the other side. He wondered if Agile'eka was there. The last time he'd seen her, she was on the opposite side and a ways behind him.

The strange place made him nervous. His keen eyes couldn't see through the thick foliage. Cautious and uneasy, he slowed his pace. Paused between each step to listen. Look. Smell. Feeling crowded and trapped—almost as he had in the plum thicket—he moved away from the tall grass and climbed toward the place where the walls of the cliff started crowding in on the valley. He found an open spot where he could see. He sat beside a big rock and watched.

To his right, there was water. More than he had ever seen before. For an instant he thought it might be the Great Water where the sun slept at night. Then he saw the other side. It wasn't the Great Water. It was a lake. The tall grass grew out a ways—the base of the stems standing in the water. When it became too deep, the stalks stopped and there was nothing but blue. So much blue that he figured it would take over a hundred running steps just to reach the far side of it. In the distance, where the canyon narrowed, giant boulders had fallen from the cliffs. Sand had washed and filtered in to fill the cracks and form a dam. It was amazing! The only water he'd seen before stood in small puddles or depressions in solid rock or . . .

Suddenly a movement caught his eye. A road-runner. At the far side of the lake, she ran, stopped, then ran a ways farther. "Thunder?" she cooed. "Thunder? Where are you?"

He stood, ruffled his feathers, and cooed back,

"Over here, Agile'eka. Way up here by this rock."

Then he saw the others who ran behind her. There were three more roadrunners. They were young—about his age. Two boy roadrunners and another girl.

"I met some new friends," Agile'eka clattered. "Come let me introduce you."

He sprang to his feet and sprinted around the lake toward them. He was so excited about meeting new friends he didn't give one thought to his feet. Until . . .

One of the boy roadrunners stopped. He tilted his head one way, then the other. "What's that weird noise?" He looked up at the sky. "There must be a storm coming."

When Thunder was almost to them, the girl roadrunner's eyes popped wide. She spread her wings and stumbled backward. The other boy veered off to the side and almost fell in the lake.

Then all three—their voices startled and astonished—gasped at the exact same instant, "OH! MY! GOSH!!!"

Chapter 12

"Don't do this," Agile'eka scolded. "You're acting like a baby."

"Am not."

"Are too."

"Am not!"

"Look at yourself," she snorted. "You're sitting out here, all alone. In the open. In the noonday sun. At least come and join us in the shade. They're really nice."

"They made fun of my feet."

Agile'eka sat down, facing him. "They didn't mean to make fun of your feet. They were just . . . just a little . . . ah . . . startled. Yeah, that's it. Startled."

Beak high, he turned away and closed his eyes. "Sounds like a storm coming," he mocked. "No wonder they named him Thunder. Thunderfoot. That's a perfect name for a bird with feet like those."

He looked back at her and didn't blink. "And they laughed at me, too."

Agile'eka leaned closer. "Not all of them. Just one. Rocket. He's kind of a smart aleck. He thinks he's really cool. But Brisk and Speedette are sweet."

She nudged him with her beak. "Look. When I first saw your feet, it startled me a bit, too. Remember? But when you told me what happened—when I got to know you . . . well, you're a pretty neat guy. I like you. They will, too. If you're nice to them, they'll be nice to you. Just give them a chance."

"No!"

"Fine!" she huffed, getting to her feet. "Just sit here on your tail feathers. I don't care. I'm going back to the shade."

It *was* getting hot out in the sun. Besides, for the past hour he'd listened to their cooing and clattering. They seemed to be having a lot of fun visiting and getting to know one another. So . . . Agile'eka had gone only a few steps when Thunder trotted after her. "Oh, all right. But if they make fun of me . . ."

The other girl roadrunner was nice—just as

Agile'eka had said. But she wasn't the brightest star in the sky. He figured that out when Agile'eka introduced them. "This is Speedette of the Sprint Clan," she said in her most formal clatter. "Speedette, this is Thunder of the Foote Clan."

The bird looked up at the sky. "Thunder? I didn't hear any thunder."

"No," Agile'eka explained. "That's his name. Thunder."

"Where? Is there lightning, too? Is it going to storm?"

"No, you don't understand. His name is Thunder. Thunder of the Foote Clan. This bird, here."

Speedette stopped looking at the sky and smiled at him. "Oh," she said with a giggle. "I'm sorry. Nice to meet you. My name is Speedette."

Then she looked back at the clear, blue sky. "You think it's going to rain?"

Agile'eka and Thunder looked at each other and rolled their eyes. Then Agile'eka introduced him to the other two. They sat in the shade and visited, Speedette still watching for clouds in the sky.

Brisk was of the Keen Clan. A month or two

older than the rest of them, he had been born far to the west of this place. When Thunder asked if he'd seen the Great Water where the sun sleeps at night, he said he hadn't. But his father had told him of it, just as Thunder's father had told him. He *had* seen the saguaro cactus and the Joshua trees, though.

The others were fascinated by his description. Speedette came from the east—even farther east than Agile'eka. Thunder asked her if she had ever seen the strange grass with the fuzzy tree limb-looking flowers. She said that they were called cattails. She added that there were a lot of them in the streams and ponds where she came from. Then she looked up at the sky. "It doesn't smell like rain. But if there's thunder . . ."

The one named Rocket yawned and preened his feathers. That's about all he'd done since they first sat to visit, always fluffing and trying to look bigger and stronger than he really was. When Thunder walked up with Agile'eka, he'd made a high-pitched clattering. It sounded like a giggle to Thunder, but he pretended not to hear.

After spending some time listening to him and watching him preen his feathers, Thunder decided that the only thing Rocket was interested in was

Rocket. They went their separate ways when the sun dropped behind the western crest of the valley. They filled up on tarantulas, and Thunder chased down a banded gecko. Just before dark, two crows swooped into the valley. They came from below the dam where the gorge was narrow. Cawing and squawking, each swooped down, snatched up a tarantula and, still making a racket, flew off again.

First thing the next morning, the crows were back. Their cawing and jabbering woke the road-runners from a peaceful sleep. But this time there were five crows, instead of just two. Others must have heard all the racket they made, because before they knew it there were ten. Fourteen. Nineteen. So many that even Brisk, who was older and wiser, couldn't keep count. Their caws and calls were almost deafening.

Fearing that there wouldn't be any tarantulas left for breakfast if they waited any longer, the five roadrunners left their high ridge to feed. Rocket raced ahead of everyone else, gobbling up the hairy-legged, fuzzy spiders as fast as he could. Thunder ate just what he needed, then returned to the shade of the rocks on the high knoll. Speedette joined him, then Agile'eka and Brisk. Rocket came waddling in, stuffed clear to his head crest. He was so full he could barely walk.

The crows left during the heat of the day. All five roadrunners rested in the shade. As it started to cool, Thunder and Brisk walked to the cattails for a drink. The water was warm, but it tasted good.

Rocket came trotting down about the time they started up the hill. "I ate too much," he groaned. He took a sip of water, then another. "Let's run or something. My tummy doesn't feel too good."

"Maybe you need to rest instead," Brisk suggested.

Rocket preened his wing feathers with his beak. "Nah. I need some exercise. Tell you what. I'll race you around the lake. Bet I can win."

With that he flapped his wings and ran in place. His feet moved so fast it sounded like a buzz on the sand instead of thumping footsteps. "Sure," Brisk said, shrugging his wings. "How about around that big cottonwood tree at the end of the cattails, across the dam, and back to the girls?"

"How about you, Thunderfoot?" Rocket called as Thunder strolled back toward the rocks.

Thunderfoot felt his head crest rise. His feet clinched the sand. Then he took a deep breath and forced himself to relax. "No, thanks," he answered calmly. "Think I'll rest a few more minutes instead."

"Ah, come on," Rocket chided. "You're not scared of losing, are you?"

Thunder ignored him and kept walking. "Maybe later," he said.

From the rocks, Thunder and the girls watched the race. Rocket led most of the way. But just after they crossed the dam, he had to stop and throw up. Thunder knew it was because he'd drunk too much water after overeating. Brisk was sitting comfortably in the shade when Rocket finally got back.

Feathers bristling and walking stiff-legged, he stomped up the hill toward them. "I want a rematch," he demanded.

Brisk shook his head. "Not now. I'm tired."

Still bristled up, Rocket turned to Thunder. "How about you . . ." He hesitated, looking down at Thunder's feet. ". . . Fatfoot?" Then, pretending it was just a slip of the tongue, he added, "Sorry, I meant Thunder . . . foot."

Thunder glared up at him. He could see the smirk on Rocket's yellow lips behind the sharp beak. *If you're nice to them, they'll be nice to you.* Agile'eka's words seemed to echo in his ears. *Just give them a chance.* As far as Thunder was concerned, Rocket had had his chance. He couldn't decide whether to hop up and kick the snot out of him with his big feet or . . .

He eased up. Smiled. "Any time you're ready."

Chapter 13

Rocket got a head start. He ran first, *then* yelled, "Go!"

It caught Thunder off guard. It made him mad. But as he chased after Rocket, the anger turned toward himself. He should have expected it from a bird like Rocket. He should have been ready.

They raced up the bank of the dry streambed. There were fallen branches and thick brush near the water. Thunder tripped a couple of times, but he didn't fall. Still, by the time they crossed the stream and started up the far side, he was way behind.

Once on the soft sand, with nothing to stumble over, he started gaining. He'd never run so hard in his life. Never wanted anything more badly than he wanted to beat this loudmouthed, obnoxious bird.

Thunder's nose was almost touching Rocket's tail when they reached the rocks and boulders that formed the dam. There he fell behind once more. His stupid feet slipped and stumbled on the uneven surface. He hated his feet!

Once on the sand he gained quickly. The sound of his heart pounded inside his head. It was almost as loud as the sound of his huge feet thundering on the dirt. There was no time to glance up and see if Agile'eka, Speedette, and Brisk were watching. He knew they were. He ran harder.

Rocket's tail feathers brushed against Thunder's wing when he caught up with him. They were side by side. Neck and neck. Beak to beak.

Watching from the corner of his eye, he felt a sudden burst of energy when he passed the other bird. He'd never felt so strong. So fast. He was winning! He was going to make it back to the rocks—first!

He was so intent on winning, Thunder thought about nothing else—saw nothing else—but the finish line. It was a second or two before he realized Rocket was no longer chasing him. There wasn't the slightest sound of his quick little feet. Rocket was gone.

Just like him, Thunder said to himself. *He knew he was losing, so he probably stopped to preen his feathers. Either that, or he's pretending to be sick so he'll have an excuse.*

Thunder glanced back. To his surprise, Rocket was still running, only he was running in the wrong direction. He was racing back toward the dam. Thunder was almost to the rocks. But there was no one to cheer him on. No Agile'eka. No Speedette. No Brisk.

A movement caught his eye. It came from behind one of the rocks. A black nose wiggled when it sniffed the air. Then Thunder saw brown fur on a long snout. Two sharp ears. Brown eyes. And the biggest, broadest head he'd ever seen.

Coyote!

Thunder was too close to stop. Just as the coyote leaped from its hiding place, he dodged to his right. There was only about ten yards of open ground, then the canyon walls rose straight up. He could never make it ahead of the coyote. So he turned right again.

The thing was huge! Close! Heavy paws almost shook the ground as the coyote closed in on the roadrunner. To Thunder's left were the trees and thick brush that lined the creek bed. His fat feet could never make it through that. He remembered the first part of the race. He'd stumbled and tripped over the twigs and limbs. Just one mistake now and the coyote would have him. He started to make another right, but from the corner of his eye, he could see the coyote almost beside him. He could see the sharp teeth. Slobber dripped from the longest ones.

There were two choices. Run for the tall thick waterweeds that Speedette called cattails, or the sandy bank around the lake. He raced straight ahead. Down the hill. Toward the lake. Coyotes are slow when they run down hill. Trouble was, roadrunners are even slower.

Thunder spread his wings. No matter how hard he flapped, he got only about eight inches off the ground. Still within easy reach of the coyote. He hit the sand, running, and tried again. This time he only got six inches of air beneath his wings.

At least it carried him to the flat near the lake. The sandy bank stretched out to his right. There were no sticks or rocks to trip over. If only . . .

The coyote must have sensed that he wanted to run that way. He stayed to Thunder's right, steadily inching his way closer as they neared the water. Now there was only one choice!

Beak forward and wings tight against his sides, Thunder charged into the cattails. He knifed between the tall blades. He could hear the coyote right behind him. It didn't knife between the blades, it crashed through them. Closer by the second. There was a strange sound beneath Thunder's big feet. A sound he'd never heard. The bottoms of his feet were hot—first from the long race around the lake, then from the sprint to escape the coyote. Now, for some reason, they felt cooler. Stronger. Faster.

Maybe. Just maybe . . .

Then he tripped. He heard the huge jaws snap behind him. Felt the pain.

Chapter 14

Once clear of the cattails, Thunder raced for the open valley. His tail hurt, but he dared not stop to see how badly he was injured. Any second the coyote would be hot on his heels again.

Right after he felt the pain in his rear end, he heard a loud, shrill yelp. There were other noises, too, sloshing and flopping and more whimpering. He didn't have time to look. Even the split second it took to glance back might mean the difference between life and death.

So he ran. Ran even faster and harder than when he was mad and racing Rocket. About a quarter of a mile from the lake, he found a dry wash that led to the top of the cliff. It was a gentle slope. At some time water had washed the sand so it was clear of rocks and sticks. He charged up and didn't slow down until he reached the top. Once there, he stopped long enough to look around and make sure there were no coyotes or bobcats. Then he turned right and ran a ways farther. An old creosote bush grew at the rim of the canyon. Tongue dangling out and mouth gaping, he gasped for air.

The shade of the creosote would be cool. A good place to watch for the coyote. A good place to rest and catch his breath.

There was still no sign of the coyote. Before Thunder sat, he took the time to inspect his rump to see how badly he was injured. Two tail feathers were missing. That was all. Of course, it still hurt. Tail feathers are big and strong, well rooted in a roadrunner's rump. The place where the coyote yanked his out was still sore. The pain really didn't matter. He was lucky just to be alive. No one knew that better than Thunder. He sat in the shade to watch.

Still no coyote.

A little ways up the valley, he could see Rocket. Watchful and nervous, he had stopped running. He perched on the very tip of a tall, sharp boulder, preening his feathers. Thunder shook his head.

It took him a minute or two to see another

movement. It was far up the valley on the opposite side. Two roadrunners were walking slowly, hopping from time to time to snatch up tarantulas or grasshoppers. They were too far away for Thunder to tell who they were. Deep in his heart, he hoped one of them was Agile'eka. She had always been nice to him. She was pretty and fun to talk with. He didn't know what he would do if the coyote had gotten her. *Where is that darned coyote?* Thunder looked near the pond. Then his eyes darted to the dry wash where he'd climbed to the top of the canyon. *Where can it be?*

"For a minute there, I thought you were smarter than I gave you credit for."

The sudden voice startled Thunder. Maybe the coyote had come straight up the canyon wall and sneaked up on him. His head whipped one way, then the other. There was nothing but the creosote bush and the desert.

"What? Who . . . who said that?"

"Move."

"Huh?"

"I said, MOVE!" Something shoved against his bottom—right on the sore spot where two of his tail feathers used to be. Thunder jumped.

Between the unexpected voice and the pain on

his rump, he jumped a little higher than he intended. A big, thick branch of the creosote shook when he clunked his head. From a hole, right where he'd been sitting, two stubby, short, clawed feet appeared. Then the edge of a shell.

"Berland!" Thunder yelped. "What are you doing here?"

Half in and half out of his burrow, the old tortoise stopped and looked up. "First off, I was watching you. Might near served yourself up to Scruffy as supper."

Thunder glanced back to the canyon. There was still no sign of the coyote. "Did he get any of my friends?" Thunder asked.

"No. They were watching. You, on the other hand, were so busy trying to beat that other roadrunner, you didn't see him until . . . well . . . if Scruffy had leaned out a little farther from behind that rock, he could have given you a kiss on the beak before you saw him. You got to watch where you're going, kid."

"Where is the coyote, anyway?"

"There," Berland snipped. "See where the cattails are moving?"

"They're all moving," Thunder snipped back. "The wind's got every single one of them waving to and fro."

"No. Look closer. There on the far side."

All the cattails leaned to the north, swaying with the gentle breeze. But one clump, near the far bank, snapped violently to the south. It sprang up and another clump beside it whacked over and threw drops of water into the air when it sprang back.

"What's he doing? Did he find something to eat in there?"

"He's stuck," Berland said with a sigh. "Stuck in the mud. Like I said, I thought you were smarter than I gave you credit for. I thought you led him in there because you knew your feet were wide enough and big enough to keep you from sinking. Scruffy, on the other hand, is the biggest coyote in these parts. Between his weight and his relatively small paws—I figured you knew he'd sink. But now I know it was just pure, dumb luck!"

Thunder tilted his head to the side and glared down at the tortoise. "What do you mean, dumb? You calling me dumb?"

Berland tilted *his* head to the side and glared right back at him. "I know your parents told you to look before you leap. They should have told you to look before you squat. Who else would plop their rump over an open burrow? Don't you know snakes love burrows and prairie dog tunnels? If I'd been a rattlesnake, well . . ."

Berland sighed and started to back into the shade of his burrow. "You're dumb, all right. But you have to be the luckiest roadrunner I ever met in all my seventy-five seasons. If that had been Tess, even dumb luck wouldn't have saved you. She'd be picking her teeth with your tail feathers."

"Berland. Wait. Who's Tess? Don't leave me. Please."

Chapter 15

Berland fussed and fumed a little, but he stayed. Thunder needed someone to talk with. Even more important, after the close call he'd had, the young roadrunner was more than ready to listen. He could tell Berland sensed that.

The old tortoise explained that Tess was the bobcat who lived down the canyon. Although she usually stayed beyond the place where the rocks had fallen to hold the water, she occasionally came to hunt in this wide part of the valley. "The crows are probably what brought the coyote," Berland said. "Crows tell other crows when there's food. When there are that many crows, and that much noise, always be on the watch for predators. Scruffy heard them and came to see what there was to eat. It's a wonder Tess didn't come to check it out, too."

He also told Thunder that Tess's paws and pads were much broader than Scruffy's. "If she had been chasing you, moving fast, she wouldn't have gotten stuck in the mud."

Thunder was just getting ready to ask Berland what mud was when he saw the coyote lunge and stumble from the edge of the cattails. He was covered from the tips of his paws to his belly with a slick, slimy, gooey coat of black. He stood for a moment, panting, then shook. Little black droplets filled the air and scattered all about. He raised his right front paw and shook it. Then his left hind paw. Then his left front, and finally his right hind. Still covered and dripping, he flopped down and started rolling.

He rolled and rubbed against the sand on one side, flipped to his back, then scraped his other side in the dirt. Once on his feet again, he walked a ways, found some dry grass, and dropped to his belly. Then he crawled and rubbed and flopped some more.

"Mud?" Thunder asked.

"Mud," Berland agreed. "It's what happens to dirt when it gets very wet. Where the cattails are, there's also decayed plant stuff mixed in. Mud can't hold you up like dry dirt. It lets you sink. Your feet were wide enough to keep you moving—as long as you ran. If you had stopped, you would have sunk in the mud and been stuck there, just like Scruffy."

Thunder watched as the coyote went back to the rocks where Speedette, Agile'eka, and Brisk had been while he and Rocket were racing. The coyote sniffed around a minute or two, but the trail was cold. So he checked out some nearby brush for a rabbit. When he found nothing, he crossed the dam and disappeared.

"I like this valley," Thunder said. "Agile'eka and I talked about living here. Raising a family of our own. We're both too young, but maybe in a year or two. Now . . . I don't know . . . Scruffy and Tess . . . maybe it's just too dangerous to claim this as our territory."

"No matter where you go in the desert it's going to be dangerous." Berland yanked his head inside his shell. "It's a harsh place. Food is hard to find—water even harder. There are always coyotes or bobcats or something that wants to eat you or bite you or sting you. This valley is a good place. There's enough food for two families of roadrunners, and no one has claimed it. When your time comes, I don't know why it shouldn't be yours. If . . ."

He poked his head out once more. "If you're smart and strong . . ."

"But I'm not very smart," Thunder confessed. "I'm not very strong, either. I tried to fly when Scruffy was chasing me, and I could barely get off the ground. My feet are too big. Too heavy to lift. I just can't—"

Suddenly Thunder felt something hitting his chest and wings. He glanced down. Sand flew at him again and again.

Berland always used his feet to dig. This time, he shoved the sand at Thunder—first with one foot, then the other. "You're just making excuses. There you go. Being lazy again."

Thunder felt his head crest bristle. "My stinking feet are huge. How can I—"

But before he could finish, Berland kicked another pawful of sand. "So your feet are huge. Big deal! So what?"

"So I can't run through brush or tree limbs. I can't fly. I can't—"

"Can't. Can't. Can't," Berland mocked. "With you, it's always 'I can't.'" He kicked another pile of sand at Thunder. "The first night we met, I told you to move. You said, 'I can't.' But you did. The next day you walked. The next day you ran. Then . . ."

He paused, glaring at Thunder out of one eye. "Then you spent a whole day pouting because you didn't like your name. Now look at you. You're big and strong. It's easy to tell you've had no trouble catching food. You're fast, too. You were beating that other roadrunner. You managed to get away from Scruffy. For someone who 'can't'—you seem to be doing pretty good. How did you get so fast?"

"I practiced," Thunder said proudly. "I ran and ran and ran. Even when I didn't need to."

"And you got stronger and faster."

With a sigh, Thunder lowered his head. His beak scraped the sand. "But I still can't fly."

"So practice that."

Thunder glanced up and shook his head. "I have! I've tried and tried. I still can't get more than eight inches off the ground. I still can't fly more than ten feet, no matter what I do. Nothing works. Nothing helps. I just don't know what to do."

Berland climbed all the way out of his burrow. He walked to the edge of the cliff, where he could see over. "I was born in this very valley," he said. "There were eight of us who hatched about the same time. We crawled from the sand—each to go our own way. I am the only one of the eight to survive.

"Two years later, I was crossing this valley. It was like today. The time when the tarantulas hatch. Before the noon sun was high, the crows filled the air. Their calls and caws were almost deafening.

"At two seasons, my shell was hard and my legs were much stronger than when I was a baby. But since I was still small, I wasn't safe from the crows. They pick up small tortoises, fly high in the air with them, then let them go to crack their shells and eat them. I was walking along, minding my own business, when one swooped down and grabbed me.

"Luckily, I was close to a rock. I caught it with both front feet and held on. That old crow lifted me—and that rock—clean off the ground. But with the rock, I was too heavy for him to get me more than an inch or so in the air. The crow tried again, but I held my rock. Another crow came, but I was still too heavy to lift. I held that rock for dear life until night came and it was safe to move on.

"What you need to do, kid, is find your rock. Then you have to practice. Train. Exercise. Get in shape. After you do that, then you need to . . ."

Way into the night, the two talked. And Thunder listened. When the morning sun climbed to the sky, Berland moved on his way. Thunder went to find Agile'eka.

Chapter 16

Agile'eka was dozing under a mesquite when Thunder first spotted her. Since he and Berland had stayed awake all night talking, he was out and about before first light. He started the search for *his* rock, even though it was almost too dark to move around.

He saw Agile'eka only an instant before she saw him. He raced toward her. She sprang to her feet. Eyes wide and head crest high, she sprinted across the flat to greet him.

They raced toward each other so fast they barely managed to stop before they crashed. So excited that she couldn't keep from hopping all around, Agile'eka rubbed her neck feathers against his.

"I thought the coyote got you," she said, her clattering almost a whimper. "You disappeared into those tall weeds. He was right on your tail feathers. I could hear him crashing around and . . . and . . . as long as he stayed in there . . . I . . . I just knew you were a goner."

He explained to her about the mud. About how his feet were big enough to keep him from sinking, but the coyote's weren't. He also told her not to try the same trick with the cattails, because with her little, dainty feet, she'd sink like a rock.

He told her about Winterfat, who was Scruffy's mate, and how they usually hunted together. But yesterday she'd stayed in their den to nurse the new pups. Then he told her about Tess.

"Bobcats are quick. They can leap almost as high as you can fly. You're not even safe in a tree," he explained. "With their long, sharp claws, they can climb higher than even the strongest roadrunner can fly."

When Agile'eka asked him how he knew all these things, he told her about Berland. Well . . . he tried to tell her about Berland. It was really hard to do, because, even though he'd described Berland to her before, she still had never seen a gopher tortoise. Neither had Speedette, who showed up about the time he was trying to explain again. They listened to Thunder's description but kept looking at each other and rolling their eyes.

"A head that looks like a snake?" Speedette asked when he finished.

"Little short legs?" Agile'eka added. "Lives inside a rock?"

"Only he calls the rock a shell? And he carries it with him wherever he goes?"

"Right." Thunder smiled. "That's it."

Smirking, both girls blinked about five times while they looked at each other. "We just don't get it. We think you're making it up. If there were such a strange animal, why haven't we ever seen it?"

Thunder puffed his chest feathers out, proud of himself for knowing the answer before they asked. "Gopher tortoises spend most of their time underground, in their burrows. Berland's territory is a seven-mile circle. One end is at the edge of the short grass prairie where I was born. The other is the ridge just above this valley. In between, he has eleven burrows. He spends his days there, when it's hot. He feeds at night. Sometimes—if he's found a lot to eat—he might spend five or six days before he moves on to the next burrow. He's like underneath the sand most of his life. That's why you never see him."

Speedette shook her head, and, spotting Brisk beside a cholla, trotted across the flats to ask him about the strange creature Thunder had described. Rocket watched from the edge of the pond, far down the valley.

Alone once more, Thunder turned to Agile'eka. He told her about his rock. What Berland had told him he needed to do so he could fly.

"What do you mean, you have to leave?" Agile'eka pouted. "I love this valley."

"I told you. I have to find my rock," Thunder explained. "I've looked all over. I can't find the right one. I have to keep searching until I find it. Will you go with me?"

Her eyes tightened. She looked at him a moment and gazed around the valley. "Why can't you stay here?"

"If I stay here," Thunder explained with a sigh, "I will not survive. If Scruffy and Winterfat come at the same time, or if Tess comes—there will be no more Thunder. But once I've found my rock, once I'm in shape, once I've trained and worked out and am ready, we can come back. Come with me. Please."

"You're leaving to go find a rock?"

"Yes."

"You're talking a rock rock? Or a rock like your friend Berland?"

"A rock rock."

She looked around again. "There are lots of rocks here. Why do you need to leave the valley to find a rock when there are so many here?"

"I haven't found *the right rock*. I started looking before light. I've searched this whole valley and the ridges on either side. It's not here."

"I really like this valley, Thunder. There's plenty to eat. We have friends here."

"As soon as I find my rock," he promised, "as soon as I'm ready . . . we'll come back."

Agile'eka hesitated a moment. And in that instant, Thunder felt his heart sink deep in his chest. She turned to him and fluttered her eyes. "I really like you, Thunder. You're nice. I think you're kind of cute, too. But . . . but . . ." she stammered. "Tell you what. You go find your rock and work out. I'll wait for you. I'll be right here when you come back. How does that sound?"

His heart was heavy. His fat feet were even heavier. They thumped the ground as he ran. The sound seemed so loud it echoed against the valley walls. It followed him to the ridge, to the mesa beyond. No matter how fast or how far he ran, the sound followed him. Almost as if repeating his name, "Thunder. Thunder. Thunder!"

Chapter 17

Three months later, and far, far from his beloved Agile'eka and their beautiful valley, Thunder's big feet didn't feel nearly as heavy. Not that they were any smaller or lighter. His feet were still huge. They still thundered on the desert floor. But everywhere Thunder went—everywhere he searched—he ran. He slowed only when sneaking up on food, or resting in the shade. As the days grew shorter, the nights cooler, his rest times became fewer and fewer.

He ran on the sand. He searched out brush and fallen limbs and ran there. Pebbles didn't bother him. He could dodge around the bigger boulders. The medium-size ones caused him to trip and stumble. So he searched out those areas and ran there. His legs were strong. So strong that he hardly noticed the weight of his big feet.

His heart—even stronger than his legs—still felt heavy. He was alone. And loneliness made his journey seem endless.

He met a few other roadrunners. Startled by the sound of his running, most raced away before he could greet them. A few laughed at him.

Sad and alone, he felt that maybe Berland had lied to him. Either that or the old tortoise was loony as a bug. Still he kept looking. Searching. At times he didn't even understand why.

The hot breath of summer gave way to the cool breezes from the north. When winter chased summer to the south, food was hard to find. The bugs must have been blown away along with the summer breeze. Snakes and lizards hid beneath the rocks or sand. Many days he went hungry. Other times he was forced to eat mesquite pods or other plants just to stay alive.

He tried not to think of Agile'eka. The memory of her only made him feel even more alone.

When spring drove winter back to the high mountains in the east—where it belonged—he finally saw what his father had called rain, the drops of water that fell from the sky. They joined together in the arroyos and chased one another, tumbling and scampering to form streams and pools. The bugs must have floated back on the drops of rain. Suddenly they seemed to be everywhere.

He had a close call with a coyote or two. Nothing he couldn't outrun or dodge. He saw a bobcat—up close and personal—for the first time. He saw the whiskers twitch only seconds before the cat leaped from behind a creosote bush. With Thunder's speed, it was all the time he needed to escape.

The sun warmed the land and it was a time of plenty again. When he saw other roadrunners, there were always two. It was the beginning of his second season. A time of new life in the desert. It made him long for Agile'eka. Made him feel more alone than ever.

"You've got to be the luckiest roadrunner in the whole wide world." That's what Berland had told him. But Thunder didn't believe that anymore. Not until he topped the crest of a high mesa . . . and tripped. He'd looked over the area—as always—to make sure there was no danger. He'd seen the cluster of stones and boulders at the edge. But he stumbled anyway.

Irritated and disgusted with himself, Thunder snapped his head around to glare at what caught his fat foot. Suddenly his eyes flashed wide. *Right size. Right shape. Give it a try.* He hopped on the rock. Eight toes wrapped about it—four on the front, four on the back. He tested it. Still gripping with his toes, he first tried to lift his right foot. The claws held. Then his left foot.

Perfect!

Hanging on tight with both feet, Thunder flapped his wings as hard as he could. When he could flap no more, he gritted his beak and flapped even harder.

He flapped so hard that he felt as if his head crest would fly clear off his skull. He strained so much that he thought his whole head might explode. Still the grip of his feet held fast.

At long last, Thunder had found *his* rock!

His heart soared with a new hope. It thumped proud and strong in his chest. Now he could dream of Agile'eka again. Now he could truly trust and *believe* everything Berland had said. The old tortoise's words—words he'd heard the night they stayed up and talked until the morning sun—surged through his head as strong and loud as his blood surged from his heart.

"With those feet of yours, you must always be watchful. See danger before danger sees you. But this is not enough. Danger is always with us in the desert. Your legs must be stronger than the fastest roadrunner. This is the only way you can escape the coyotes and bobcats. And before you can return to this place—the valley where Tess lives— you must fly. Your feet are heavy. So to fly, your wings must be stronger and more powerful than any roadrunner's.

"I will tell you how to do this. First you must find your rock. If it is too small, with those big feet you won't be able to get a grip on it. If it is too big, your claws will slip and not hold. It must be *your* perfect rock.

"Next you must practice. Every day, you must try to lift the rock from the ground. You don't really have to lift it, but you do have to try your hardest. This is the only way to make your wings strong enough to fly with those feet of yours. You will know when you are ready. Then and only then will it be time to return."

Now that Thunder had finally found *his* rock, now that his search was done, he knew, without a doubt, that it would be no time at all before he could return to the valley.

One day turned to three. Three days to a week. A week to a month. Spring to summer. Summer to fall. Fall to winter. Until finally, Thunder could fly.

Chapter 18

Before Thunder landed next to the yucca bush, he thought the roadrunner was dead. Chin and beak resting on the sand, she lay perfectly still. She didn't look around for danger. She didn't even blink.

She looked too young to have died from old age. There were no teeth or claw marks that he could see. *Probably a rattlesnake,* he decided. But when he dropped his rock and landed a few feet from the bush with the long, sharp, pointed leaves, she blinked and raised her head from the sand.

"What's with the rock?"

Her voice was weak. Sad. Thunder glanced over his wing. Then, pretending not to see the rock, he glanced over the other wing. "Rock? What rock?"

She shot him a disgusted look before she lowered her head to the sand once more. "The rock you just dropped," she said, sighing. "I've never seen a roadrunner flying around with a rock. What are you doing with it?"

For a second he wanted to tell her that he was taking it back to show Berland. He wanted to tell her how he'd practiced and trained. How surprised he was, the first day his wings were strong enough actually to lift the rock from the ground. And how he wasn't satisfied just to lift it. He needed to carry it. Lift it high into the air and fly with it.

Even that wasn't enough. He'd decided to take it with him to the valley. Besides, if he quit working out his wings might get weak again. He couldn't risk that, so . . .

But he didn't even know this girl. So he lied. "Oh, *that* rock. Well . . . ah . . . er," he stammered. "It's just a rock I found. I kinda liked it. You know . . . it's like my favorite rock. I just carry it around for . . . ah . . . for . . . good luck. Yeah, that's it. Good luck."

Dust puffed from either side of her beak when she let out a little snort. Then she closed her eyes once more.

"What's with you?" Thunder asked.

"Nothing."

"Are you sick?"

"No."

"Hurt?"

"No."

"Got bit by a rattlesnake, didn't you?"

"No."

He frowned down at her. "Then why are you lying around like you're half dead? Winter's here. Food's hard to find. You should be out hunting."

"I haven't eaten in two days," she said.

"Can't find any food?"

"No. I'm just not hungry. I'm depressed."

Thunder's beak fell open. "Depressed?"

"Yeah, depressed," she snapped. "You probably don't even know what that means."

Thunder looked down. He lifted a foot and shook it in her face. He wanted to say, "With feet like these, you can bet your sweet little tail feathers I know what depressed means!" Only when she looked at his foot—and didn't act startled or shocked, but just closed her eyes again—all he could say was, "Why are you depressed?"

"I got dumped," she said.

"Dumped?"

"My boyfriend dumped me!" she sniffed. "He told me he loved me. He told me I was the only one. He said he'd come back. Four days ago, when it warmed up, I thought it was spring. I thought he would return. He didn't."

"Maybe something happened to him. Maybe a coyote, or a bobcat, or . . . something got him."

"Yeah, something got him all right!" she scoffed. "When he didn't come for me, I went to find him. He's already got a mate. Two valleys over. They raised their first family last season. He didn't even tell me. He lied to me."

"The guy sounds like a real jerk. What's his name, anyway?"

"Rocket."

Thunder's head crest bristled. His eyes popped wide. "Rocket? Always preening his feathers? Smart mouth?"

"Oh, so you know the guy?"

Thunder felt a chill run from his tail to his neck. "We've met. You didn't happen to find out who his mate was? You didn't happen to hear her name?"

"No. I did see her, though. I watched them for a while from the ridge above their valley. She's very pretty. Lots prettier than me. I'm just ugly. Homely."

"You're not homely," Thunder protested. "You'd actually be kinda cute if you weren't moping around."

The bird just looked at him. "She's *pretty*. She's

mature, and a good hunter, too. You know. Quick. Agile."

Another chill swept through Thunder. It was so cold and so deep that he trembled all over. It took a while before he could even speak. Finally he chased the thought from his mind. "Why are you wasting your time over a bum like Rocket? Forget him."

"I can't," she sniffed. "I love him so."

Thunder talked with her until it was almost dark. He tried to cheer her up. Tried to reason with her. Nothing seemed to work. No matter what he said, no matter what he tried, she wouldn't budge from under the yucca plant. The idea, or maybe it was more of a memory, hit him when he glanced at his rock and thought about Berland. He got to his feet, strolled over, hopped on the rock, and latched on with his claws. "Move."

She opened an eye. "What?"

"MOVE!"

"Why?"

"I've got to be on my way. It takes a few feet to get this rock clear off the ground. I don't want to hit you."

She sighed and dropped her head back to the sand. "It doesn't matter if you hit me or not. I just don't have the will to live."

Thunder rolled his eyes. He flapped his power-ful wings. Lifted the rock straight up. "Maybe I'll see you around, kid," he called. "That is, IF you get off your lazy tail feathers and do something. You know, like hunt, or run, or eat. 'Course, you keep sitting there, feeling sorry for yourself, I'll see you in about a month or so. When I come back this way. Well . . . I won't really see you. I'll just see what's left of your lazy carcass after the buzzards and the fire ants are through with it."

With that he swooped right over her and flew on his way. From behind him, out of the very corner of one eye, Thunder saw her head snap up. Her sad eyes narrowed to tiny, angry slits. Her head crest arched high.

"LAZY??!"

Chapter 19

There was a large barrel cactus on the floor of his valley. Since there was more than one barrel cactus, and since it was dark, it took him a while to find the right one, the one where Berland had told him he usually stayed during the winter. It was dark when he dropped the rock next to the burrow. *That ought to get his attention.* Thunder felt a sly grin tug behind his beak.

He sniffed the burrow before he sat on top of it, remembering how Berland had warned him that rattlers loved burrows or prairie dog tunnels. There was no smell of rattlesnake. There was no smell of Berland, either. *It's winter. He should be here. Unless . . .*

The burrow on the ridge of the canyon was the last place Thunder had seen his old friend. Berland told him that he went there only when it rained. That was because sometimes the stream on the valley floor overflowed and ran too close to his winter burrow. *Surely it's not going to rain. It's too cold.*

For a minute, Thunder thought about going up there, just to see. Then he decided against it. It was dark. Besides, the air that blew from the tops of the mountains was so thick and heavy it felt even colder than normal. No matter how strong he had become, cold was still cold.

It didn't rain that night. Always watchful, Thunder did see the white crystals. First they drifted from the sky. They floated one by one to the sand. Then they came faster, swirling and gliding through the air. Hours before daylight they filled the night sky—so thick and white he could hardly see his beak in front of his face.

"It is called snow." His father had told him of it, but he had never seen it. Thunder's father had heard of snow from his father, who had never seen it either. Not even once in their lives.

Thunder was the first in three generations. He stayed awake, all night, watching the strange and marvelous feathers of white that filled the desert.

When first light came he eased from the cover of the barrel cactus and shook his feathers. The sparkling white covered the valley floor, the cactus, the cholla. The strange crackling sound beneath his feet made him smile. He wanted to run. Listen to it. Feel it crunch beneath his—

Thunder hadn't taken his first stride when he saw the movement. He froze. Two roadrunners sat on the lowest branch of a mesquite tree. Another large branch, higher up, had given them a little shelter. The male shook his feathers and began to preen. "I can't believe this stuff. It's nasty. My feathers are all wet."

He griped and fussed as he preened. "I'm a total mess. I must look a fright."

"Now, Rocket," Agile'eka cooed, "don't get yourself all in a fizz. You look as handsome as always. Here. Let me help you."

She preened his neck feathers. Rubbed her beak, lovingly, against his chest. Thunder stood totally still. He *couldn't* move. His heart was frozen—colder than the snow beneath his feet. Agile'eka's promise to wait for him had been a lie. His true love had found another.

All was lost. All the searching. All the training. All the running and lifting and flying. It was all for nothing.

Thunder eased down until his feathers rested in

the snow. Feeling deserted, betrayed, and even scorned, he would hide here. Stay totally still until they went away. Then he'd slip off. Unseen. He'd take his broken heart back to the high mesa. There to live, alone, and never be seen by either of them again. He'd—

Another movement. Behind him. He had to turn his head to see. It was Brisk, with Speedette running right beside him. They weren't really running, though. Not for roadrunners. They were stumbling and jerking and lunging. Their feet sank in the deep snow. A huge male coyote and a smaller female were hot on their heels.

Scruffy and Winterfat were having trouble running in the snow, too. But not nearly as much trouble as Speedette and Brisk. With each leap and lunge, they gained on the two roadrunners. His friends were goners.

Thunder ran. That's what roadrunners do. That is what every instinct, every fiber of his being told him to do. The Law of the Desert. Survive. There was no thud or sound of thunder as he ran. Just a light crunch and crackle as the snow compressed beneath his weight. As if he were running on fine sand, his enormous feet barely broke the surface. There were no twigs to trip him. No pebbles or rocks to stub his toes on.

He'd never run so fast before. Rocket and Agile'eka were still preening when he shot past the mesquite. Behind him, Thunder could hear their clattering. "You hear something?" Agile'eka asked.

"I think so," Rocket answered. "I thought I saw something, too. But it went by so fast I'm not sure."

"It wasn't a roadrunner, was it?" she wondered.

"No." Rocket kept preening. "I can see Brisk and Speedette. There aren't any other roadrunners in our—"

Suddenly his clattering was high-pitched and terrifying. "It's Winterfat and Scruffy! They're right behind Speedette. They're coming this way! RUN!!!"

Thunder glanced back. The coyotes were closing in. Another five or six leaps and Speedette . . .

It's a shame, he thought. *She wasn't very bright, but she was nice. She never made fun of my feet. She had a sweet disposition. Nasty old coyotes. I ought to . . .*

Another thought scampered through his head, stopping the first one. It was as if two voices were arguing inside of him. He could almost hear his father's voice—the day this parents had found him beneath the creosote bush: *At The Naming, you must be on your own. We can no longer help you. You cannot help us. It is the Rule. If something happens to me, your mother must survive. She must find another so the roadrunner will continue.*

And his mother's voice, soft and cooing inside his head, answering, *He doesn't yet have his name. Maybe it would not be breaking the Rule of Nature. Perhaps we could just bend it a little.*

The only thing faster than a roadrunner's feet is his mind. The thoughts, the memories of Mama and Daddy bringing him grasshoppers, lizards, scorpions . . . the memory of Rocket laughing at him . . . of Agile'eka not laughing . . . All these things and more flashed through his head in less than two strides of his big feet. And on the third stride . . .

Chapter 20

Sheets of white billowed into the crisp air when Thunder leaned sharply to the side, and set his feet. The plume of snow hadn't even begun its downward fall to the desert floor, when . . .

He spun and charged! Chances were that neither coyote had ever been charged by a roadrunner. Fact is, they'd probably never seen a roadrunner from this angle before—only from behind while chasing it. The sight of one racing toward him like an angry hornet must have startled and confused Scruffy. He slowed and veered off to the left.

Winterfat, on the other hand, was closer to Speedette than Scruffy had been to Brisk. She was so intent on a plump, juicy roadrunner for breakfast that she didn't even see Thunder coming.

When he darted between Speedette and Brisk,

they didn't slow down, they didn't look at him, they didn't so much as blink. Eyes wide with the panic of imminent death, they just ran.

Winterfat didn't look at him, either. Her eyes were focused only on the tail feathers that were almost within reach. When the sharp, hard beak stabbed her right behind her ear, she *did* yelp, though. Angry and hurt, she snarled and snapped. As fast as Thunder ran on the soft powder, he was past her tail before she even felt the pain, much less turned to bite at whatever had caused it. From the corner of his left eye, he could see her reel to the side, stumble, and plow head over heels into the snow. Her speed rolled her a couple of times before she staggered to her feet again and shook the snow off.

From the other eye, Thunder saw Scruffy. Finally recognizing the strange thing as prey, the coyote snarled, licked his lips, and leaped. Thunder dodged and ran—not very fast at first, not until he was sure Winterfat was after him, too.

Once certain that both coyotes were after him and no longer chasing his friends, Thunder took off! His strong legs . . . his wide feet . . . the soft powder . . . it was as if he was running on the very air itself.

Trouble was, he ran *too* fast. A crow's caw made him glance back. When he realized the coyotes were no longer following, he slowed, then turned to look. Two crows sat at the very top of an old cottonwood tree. Brisk and Speedette were halfway up the canyon wall to his right. Using their wings, they leaped and hopped from one boulder to the next, working their way up the sheer rock face toward the safety of the ridge.

Deciding they had no chance of catching something that ran so fast they could barely see it, Scruffy and Winterfat had turned back to go after easier prey. Thunder could see them running toward the lake. They had spotted the preening lovebirds!

But Agile'eka and Rocket had seen them, too. They were already on the move, running for the big rocks that held the lake.

Agile'eka reached the dam first. She hopped and scampered across the rocks. Rocket hopped, but he didn't scamper. His feet slipped on the first boulder. He fell, hitting with such a thud that Thunder could almost feel it halfway up the canyon.

Rocket staggered to his feet and ran. But he didn't follow Agile'eka across the dam. He ran to the right. At the canyon wall, he turned and ran left. At the lake he turned and ran again, but this time, confused and disoriented, he ran back straight toward the two coyotes.

"I got this one," Scruffy yelped. He pointed his sharp nose at the streambed. "Head that one off at the pass."

Winterfat crossed the dry creek bed and headed to the far side of the cattails. Thunder took off, even faster than he had when the coyotes were after him. The long, green leaves of the cattails were brown and limp with the winter cold. Scruffy was almost to them, headed east. From the other direction, and headed west, Rocket was just about to the place where the cattails stopped in the deep water. Even as fast as he was, Thunder knew he couldn't get there in time. So . . . he took to the air.

Mouth open, slobber dripping in anticipation of the meal he was about to catch, Scruffy was less than ten yards from Rocket when Thunder landed and trotted up beside him. The coyote spotted him out of the corner of his eye and reached to snap.

Thunder took one stride to the side—just enough to escape the sharp teeth. Two more strides moved him ahead of the big coyote. Once there he cut right in front of him and darted toward the cattails. Scruffy was the biggest coyote Thunder had ever seen. He also had to be the dumbest. Darned if that old coyote didn't follow him right into the cattails, just like he'd done the last time they met.

Behind him Thunder heard the squishing, sloshing sound of wet mud. Then the yelp when Scruffy's paws sank and he realized he was stuck. Finally there was the snarling and lunging and splashing as the coyote struggled to yank himself free.

At the far edge of the cattails, Thunder paused. Not long enough to sink in the mud, just long enough to look before he leaped. Winterfat wasn't waiting for him there. She was still after Agile'eka, who ran near the wall of the canyon, trying to skirt around the coyote and make it to the wide part of the valley.

Once outside the cattails and away from the soft mud, Thunder could see that the coyote had the angle on Agile'eka. She would cut her off near the straight, flat cliffs, just before the valley widened. The rocks there were tall—taller than a roadrunner could fly. They also sloped back into the base of the ridge, forming a box canyon. There would be no place for Agile'eka to run.

Thunder sprinted toward her. Winterfat was only a few yards from Agile'eka when he sprang into the air. Just above and a little behind, he folded his wings tight against his side, aimed his huge feet right at the back of Winterfat's skull, and . . .

Chapter 21

"My hero!"

The voice was so loud it shook a little clump of snow from a bare creosote branch just above Thunder's head. He gave a snort. Blowing it off his beak, he glanced up.

Agile'eka raced toward him. Rocket was headed his way, too. He was a bit behind because he kept stopping to preen his feathers. "You are so brave, Thunder." Agile'eka swooned. "You are so wonderful. My hero."

She rushed to his side, fluttered her eyelashes, and rubbed her cheek against his neck feathers. Thunder didn't even bother to get up. "That was like totally awesome," Rocket cooed as he strutted up. "I mean, the way you landed on that coyote's head. Hit her so hard it jammed her nose clear under the snow. I never saw a coyote flip over and land on her back before. Neat trick, man. You'll have to teach me how to do that one of these days."

Thunder just sighed and shook his head. Agile'eka sat down and nestled against his wing. "I'm so glad you came back to me. I thought you might never return. I've waited so long. Now we can . . ."

"Waited so long?" Thunder repeated, arching his eyebrows.

Agile'eka blinked. "Yes. You've been gone over a season and . . ."

"And you waited for me? All this time?"

"Well . . . I . . . ah . . ." She stopped stammering long enough to clear her throat. "None of that matters now. You're back. Now we can be together again—forever."

Frowning, Rocket strutted up, preened a wing feather, and looked at her. "What about us?" he asked.

Agile'eka ignored him. Rubbed her beak against Thunder's wing. "Thunder is the bravest, strongest roadrunner in all the world. I want him!"

When Thunder stood, he gave her a little nudge to get her off the wing she was rubbing. Since his wings were stronger than he thought, the little nudge almost sent her rolling. "Trouble is," Thunder said, "I don't want you."

"You don't want me?" Agile'eka gasped, her beak gaping wide in disbelief.

Thunder smiled and shook his head. "Nope."

Eyes tight, she bristled and stared at him—but for only a moment. "Come on, Rocket," she snapped, turning toward him and stomping off. "I hate this valley. Coyotes. Bobcats. Now it's overcrowded. Too many roadrunners."

"But . . . but . . ." he stammered.

"Oh, shut up, Rocket. Quit preening. And come on!"

Thunder watched as they walked toward a hill to the west. It had been a long day. The noon sun was high. Most of the snow was gone from the valley. All that was left of it were stripes and patches in the shade. He sat down to relax. No sooner had he settled beneath the bush, when something nudged his foot.

"MOVE!"

Startled, he sprang straight up. Snapping branches with his powerful hop, he crashed through the creosote bush and landed at the very top. Looked down.

There was a digging sound. Snow caved in beneath the footprints where he sat. Berland's head, feet, and shell popped through. "Guess you're a little smarter than I gave you credit for, kid."

"Huh?"

"Getting rid of Agile'eka. Smart move. You hadn't been gone a day when she started flirting with Brisk. When he wouldn't have anything to do with her, she started in on Rocket. And even after they hitched up, she was after every roadrunner who happened to wander through this valley. Never seen anything like that gal. You're better off without her."

"I know," Thunder said with a sigh, hopping down to sit beside his friend. Still . . . inside . . . he felt a bit sad and lonely.

"So how you been doing? Looks like you've been eating well. Ever find your rock?"

"Yes. It took me a while, but I found it."

"Been practicing your flying?"

Thunder would show Berland. He knew the old tortoise would be impressed and proud of him. He might even wait a little while, go get his rock, and drop it beside the burrow so Berland could see for himself. But not right now. So all he said was, "I practiced some."

Frowning, Berland glanced back toward the valley. "What's with all the crows? When I crawled in my burrow last night, there were two sitting in that cottonwood, across the creek. Now there's eight or nine of those noisy things."

Thunder hadn't even noticed until Berland mentioned it. Berland tilted his head to the side, listening. "That's the trouble with crows," he said. "With all of 'em trying to talk at the same time, makes 'em darned hard to understand. Something about an eagle who can run faster than a coyote."

Berland laughed. "That's the most ridiculous thing I ever heard. Eagles and hawks are great in the air, but they can barely hop on the ground, much less run. You seen Speedette and Brisk?"

"On the ridge over there." Thunder pointed with his beak.

Berland stretched his neck. "Looks like they're watching something down by the cattails. Oh, it's Winterfat. She's got a bloody nose. Wonder what happened to her."

"Must have bumped into something."

About then, another coyote came stumbling and

sloshing out of the cattails. Black, gooey, sloppy mud dripped from his belly and haunches. Berland frowned at him. Then he turned and frowned at Thunder. "You didn't let Scruffy chase you across those cattails again, did you? Not while Winterfat was around. Don't you know how dangerous that is? What if she'd circled the cattails and had been there waiting for you?"

"She didn't even see me," Thunder said. "She was busy with something else."

They sat for a while, Thunder resting, Berland trying to listen to the crows and figure out what all the chatter was about. When he noticed Thunder staring longingly at the hill to the west, he glanced that way too. Agile'eka and Rocket were almost to the top. Almost out of sight.

"Do kind of feel sorry for Rocket," Berland said.

"Don't bother," Thunder snorted. "He's just as bad as she is. I met this girl roadrunner a couple of valleys back. She thought Rocket was her boyfriend. He'd told her he wanted to be her mate. They'd raise a family together. Didn't bother to tell her he already had a mate. Don't feel sorry for him. Rocket and Agile'eka deserve each other."

"What was her name?"

Thunder frowned. "Whose name?"

"The girl you met."

Thunder thought a moment, then shrugged. "Don't think I got her name."

"Was she kind of plump? Cute face? Long legs?"

Thunder shrugged. "Cute face, all right. Never did see her legs. She was sittin' on 'em—feeling sorry for herself because Rocket dumped her. But she definitely wasn't plump. Fact is she was so depressed she hadn't eaten in two days. If she didn't get up and hunt, she may not have made it."

Berland's neck stretched farther than Thunder had ever seen. He squinted. Frowned. "Maybe she's not plump. Maybe she's just got her feathers all ruffled. Maybe she's just mad." He looked back at Thunder. "Think you might be in trouble, kid."

Once Thunder found what Berland was talking about, once he saw the roadrunner walking down the valley, once his head was pointed in the right direction, not only could he see her, he could hear her, too.

"Where do you get off calling me lazy?" she clattered. Only the clattering was so loud and shrill and mad it sounded more like the call of a screech owl. "And don't even try to hide from me! I know you're down here. I found that stupid rock you were carrying around. Sooner or later, I'm gonna find you. And when I do . . ."

Suddenly, Berland's head and front legs drew inside his shell. "Oh, no!" the old tortoise gasped. "It's Tess!"

Chapter 22

His eyes were keener than any other roadrunner's. He was more watchful than any other roadrunner. Still Thunder had not seen a movement. The wind hadn't blown. The air was still as death itself—not even the slightest breath to twitch the long whiskers or wiggle the sharp tufts of hair at the peaks of the ear. The crows didn't even tell.

But they did show him where Tess was. Seven cottonwoods lined the dry streambed. Crows cawed and jabbered in only six of them. On a low branch, behind the gnarled trunk of the farthest tree, Thunder saw the pointed ear. A yellow eye peeked around the trunk. Totally motionless. Waiting for the angry roadrunner to get just . . . a little . . . closer.

"No!" Berland said when Thunder got to his feet.

"It's too late, kid. Even the fastest roadrunner couldn't run that far in time to warn her."

Thunder crouched. "I know."

With that, he sprang into the sky. There was movement. From high above the cottonwood tree, Thunder finally saw it. Cats usually wiggle their rear ends right before they pounce. The stub tail twitched. Thunder's powerful wings clamped tight against his sides. Aimed for the soft spot, right where the little, stub tail joined Tess's backbone.

"Come out and face me, you coward." The girl roadrunner was almost to the tree, oblivious to the bobcat, and still yelling. "You can't hide from me forever. And when I find you . . ."

Her back compressed and tight as a coiled spring, the bobcat leaped! Sharp front claws reached out—aiming where her prey was. Hind legs exploded.

Faster than a bolt of lightning chasing a spring storm, Thunder dived from the sky. An instant before Tess's hind feet left the limb where she hid, his sharp beak struck!

Tess snarled and squalled. The impact threw her jump off. She intended to land on the young roadrunner. Instead, the sudden pain sent her flying straight—right into another branch of the cottonwood.

Small limbs snapped as she broke through them. Stub tail and back spinning, she managed to catch a large limb with the very tips of her claws.

Thunder hopped to the limb beside her. Cat eyes, full of anger and hate, glared up at him. Thunder smiled down at her. Then he pecked the back of her paw.

When she yanked it away, Tess lost what little grip her claws had on the branch. Hissing and spitting, she fell.

Cats always land on their feet. Thunder had heard that someplace . . . from someone. That's why it kind of surprised him when Tess hit flat on her back. She yowled again when a sharp stone stabbed her.

The girl roadrunner was gone. She streaked across the creek and ran for the far ridge. Tess lay still for quite a while. Finally, she managed to roll over and get to her feet. Crows cawed and laughed. Flipping her tail, the bobcat strolled back toward the lower canyon as if nothing had happened. Thunder waited until he was sure she was gone, then he flew back to join his friend.

For the first time in his life, Berland was

speechless. He stood there, mouth agape, staring at Thunder for a long, long . . . really long . . . time. At last he closed his mouth and cleared his throat. "Does the word 'overachiever' mean anything to you?" he asked.

Thunder shrugged his wings. "Not really. What does it mean?"

"Okay, kid. When I told you about finding the rock to hold on to while you practiced flapping your wings, I meant just make them strong enough to get those big feet of yours off the ground. You know—so you could get away from predators. I didn't say anything about circling around like a buzzard in the sky. Then you do a nosedive like a falcon. On top of that, you attack a bobcat! Roadrunners *do not* attack bobcats or . . . or . . ."

He stopped jabbering a moment to stare. "That eagle the crows were talking about . . . the one that can run faster than a coyote . . . that, ah . . . that wouldn't happen to be you, would it?"

Thunder shrugged again. All Berland could do was roll his eyes and shake his head.

"There you are!"

Thunder and Berland both jerked and looked around. "I knew I'd find you! How dare you call me lazy! I'll have you know that yesterday I caught three mice. This morning I chased down a kangaroo rat. He was huge and could run and hop like a jackrabbit. No *lazy* roadrunner could do that. Just where do you get off calling me—"

Thunder raised his head crest and flapped. The wind that raced from beneath his powerful wings fluttered her ruffled feathers. "Excuse me," he interrupted. "Do you realize that I just saved your life? The least you could do is say, 'Thank you.'"

Her ruffled feathers smoothed. She stood very straight. "I am sorry. Just because you have no manners doesn't mean I should be rude, too. Thank you."

"You're welcome," Thunder said with a smile.

"But if you think all that flopping and flying around impressed me, you're badly mistaken," she squawked. "Carrying that stupid rock around. That's crazy. I bet I could find *me* a rock or two, and with a little practice I could do just as well as you. Better even!"

Thunder ruffled *his* feathers. "What do you mean no manners?"

"You told me to quit feeling sorry for myself, and get up off my LAZY tail feathers," she huffed. "That's just downright rude!"

"But when you said you were ugly or homely, I

also told you I thought you were cute. Remember?"

"I remember." Her feathers ruffled again, making her look almost twice as big. "I bet every girl you meet, you tell *her* how BEAUTIFUL *she* is. With me it's . . . CUTE! Thanks a lot."

Thunder shrugged his wings. "Well . . . I like cute."

"Kid's got a temper, doesn't she?" Berland whispered from beside him.

"Sure does," Thunder whispered back, "but she is kinda cute."

"That's rude, too," she snapped.

"What?" Thunder stepped back, almost hiding behind Berland.

"Whispering. You and . . . and your friend . . ." She arched an eyebrow and glared down at the tortoise.

Berland, who didn't appreciate being stuck between the two, had drawn his neck part way inside his shell. "Pardon me for not introducing myself," he said, sticking his neck out once more. "My name is Berland."

"Pleasure to meet you, Berland," she said politely.

"And your name?" he asked.

Suddenly her ruffled feathers began to flatten. She turned her head. "I'm Berland," the tortoise repeated. "And you are . . . ?"

There was a long . . . LONG . . . silence. The girl roadrunner took a step or two, as if to walk away, then sank to sit on the ground. Ducking her head and not looking at either of them, she answered, "Tripsalot of the Racer Clan."

"Tripsalot?" Thunder asked.

Still not looking at either of them, she sighed. "When I was little, I was sort of clumsy. My parents didn't think I had a chance to survive. The day of The Naming, I got kind of excited. I was chasing a dragonfly and stumbled over my own stupid feet. They named me the only thing they could. Tripsalot."

"And what is his name?" Crows cawed from above. "What is *his* name?" Others joined in. "What is his name? Tell us *his* name!"

Thunder didn't look at them. Instead, he stepped right over Berland and sat down beside Tripsalot. "Hi," he cooed softly. "My name is Thunder of the Foote Clan. It's nice to meet you . . . again. You want to go find something to eat?"

"I don't know." She gave a little snort.

"His name is Thunderfoot!" The crows screamed as they flew away.

Thunder leaned closer. "We could hang out a little. Get to know one another. Might be fun."

She snorted again. "Well, first off you're not that handsome. And all that flying around . . . I bet you're just a showoff. And . . . and . . ."

He got to his feet and smiled down at her. "There are lots of dragonflies near the cattails. Come on."

Finally, she shrugged her wings and stood beside him. "Oh, all right. Guess it's better than sittin' home alone to rot."

It wasn't much of a compliment. *This might be more of a challenge than learning how to fly,* Thunder thought to himself. He smiled anyway, because she WAS kinda cute. Berland slipped quietly and unnoticed into his burrow.

The End (Maybe)

Still hidden behind the mesquite tree with the wide trunk, Thunder leaned toward his friend. He wanted to ask, again, if the old tortoise remembered. But as their eyes met, the look told him there was no need. Memories of a lifetime had spun through their heads in those few moments. Memories of friendship, and trust, and . . .yes . . . even love, were clear as the blue desert sky.

Berland smiled at Thunder. Thunder smiled back.

"Some say they still live in their Valley of Paradise," the father roadrunner continued, his three children listening to his every word. *"Others say that a giant eagle tried to steal one of their babies. They chased him to the sky. Chased him past the moon, beyond*

the sun, clear above the stars. And they are still chasing them to this very day.

"The name of Thunderfoot is sacred. No other roadrunner will ever be given that name, from now until the end of time. The name Tripsalot is also revered. No other roadrunner will ever be given that name.

"The legend of the greatest roadrunners must be remembered. It must be passed down from one generation to the next."

"That's it," Thunder whispered. "Flew past the moon and the sun to chase an eagle. This is the stupidest, most unbelievable story I've ever heard.

"First off, I didn't grab that bobcat and fly up in the air with her. I just kinda nudged her off that branch. And nobody smashed a bobcat with a boulder. Tess came back only three or four more times. The first time, I dropped my rock close to her, and she ran off. The next time, I was sitting on our nest. Tripsalot had been practicing her flying, too. She grabbed her two rocks and dropped both of them. One of them hit Tess, but it didn't hurt her all that much." He looked at Berland and shook his head. "Where do they get all this stuff?"

"They got it from Tess and Winterfat and

Scruffy. Brisk, Speedette, even Rocket and Agile'eka told. The crows were there, too. Remember? The legend has spread through the entire desert."

Thunder gave a snort and started to his feet. "I'm gonna put an end to it, right now. I'm gonna—"

Berland reached out and put his foot on top of Thunder's. "Please don't."

In the fourteen seasons Thunder had known the old tortoise, he had never *asked*. He always told. This time his voice was soft—almost pleading. Even the touch of his foot on Thunder's big toes was tender.

Silently. Slowly. The roadrunner settled behind the mesquite trunk to sit beside his old friend. "Why not?" he wondered.

"We all need heroes," Berland offered with a gentle smile. "What would this old world be like without legends and folk tales and . . . heroes?"

Thunder took a deep breath and sighed. "But flying beyond the moon and the sun and the stars— that's stupid. It can't be done. It makes me sound bigger than life. All those things . . . all the stuff the father told those kids . . . it's just impossible."

Berland stretched his neck so far out his nose almost touched Thunder's beak. "The truth is even more impossible. You and Tripsalot have been together for fourteen seasons. Most roadrunners live only between six and eight. You are no giant. You never were. You're just an ordinary roadrunner. Well . . . ordinary except for those big feet. You had trouble walking, running, and you couldn't fly worth a flip. Every time I asked you, suggested to you, or even told you to do something, the only response I ever got was 'I can't.'

"Now, even at your age, you run like the wind. You taught your mate about the rocks. How many roadrunners do you know who chase coyotes or drop rocks on bobcats? It's impossible. It can't be done. Right?

"If they knew the truth—the whole story—every time a young roadrunner said, 'I can't,' his parents would wash his mouth out with Stink Bug juice. 'I can't' would be like bad words.

"Let the roadrunner tell the legend. Let the roadrunner children listen and pass it on to their children. Let them keep their hope, their belief . . . their hero."

"Now that you have heard the Legend of Thunderfoot," the proud father roadrunner announced, *"It is time for The Naming.*

"When your mother and I say, 'Go!' you will race into the desert, find food, and bring it back to show us. We will watch. When you return, a name will be given.

"Ready. Set . . ."

Thunder and Berland watched as, each in turn, the three young roadrunners raced off into the desert. With their parents watching, facing the other direction, it was the perfect time for the old friends to slip from their hiding place and head back to their valley. They waited until they were far from the roadrunner family before they spoke.

"How is Tripsalot, anyway?" Berland asked.

"She's doing fine. I'm not sure about me, though."

"What do you mean?"

"Well, I left her sitting on our eggs." Thunder flinched. "I told her I was going with you for a little while. Didn't know we were going to be gone all night."

Berland smiled back over his shell. "Kid's still got a temper, huh?"

"Boy, does she!" Thunder nodded. "I'm surprised I've got any tail feathers left—the way she's always chewin' on my rear end."

"Why don't you go on ahead," Berland suggested. "I'll catch up after a while."

Thunder smiled back at him. "No. Think I'll stay with you. Haven't seen you in a couple of full moons. Got some visiting to catch up on. Besides, I think she *enjoys* fussing at me. Gives her something to do."

Berland stopped and gave a little chuckle. "If she gets too mad, we'll just tell her the Legend of Thunderfoot. Surely she won't chew the tail feathers off a living legend."

Thunder laughed. "With her temper? Don't count on it."

About the Author

BILL WALLACE is the author of several beloved books for young readers, including *A Dog Called Kitty*, *Snot Stew*, *Goosed!*, and *No Dogs Allowed!*. He has won twenty state awards, as well as the Arrell Gibson Lifetime Achievement Award for Children's Literature from the Oklahoma Center for the Book.

A former classroom teacher, principal, and physical education teacher, he is now a full-time author and public speaker. He lives in Chickasha, Oklahoma, with his wife and sometime writing partner, Carol.